THAT MAN FROM TEXAS

The townsfolk didn't care about Jubal Wills' color when they hired him. They just cared about the reputation that had traveled up from the lawless plains of Texas to the wide-open Montana range— the legend of a black man who could come out on top in any fight with any man, be he black, white or red. So the good people of Yellowstone City sent for Jubal and pinned a star on his chest. Then they sat back and watched as a ruthless clan of Southern rednecks rode into town with guns at the ready and blood-lust in their eyes. Now Jubal was going to have to live up to his name—or die trying . . .

THAT MAN FROM TEXAS

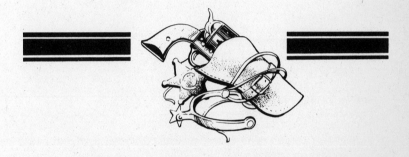

Steven C. Lawrence

ATLANTIC LARGE PRINT
Chivers Press, Bath, England.
John Curley & Associates Inc.,
South Yarmouth, Mass., USA.

Library of Congress Cataloging in Publication Data

Lawrence, Steven C.
  That man from Texas.

  (Atlantic large print)
  1. Large type books.   I. Title.
[PS3562.A916T5 1986]   813'.54   85–14913
ISBN 0–89340–953–7 (Curley: lg. print)

British Library Cataloguing in Publication Data

Lawrence, Steven C.
  That man from Texas.—Large print ed.—
  (Atlantic large print)
  Rn: Lawrence D. Murphy   I. Title
  813'.54[F]   PS3562.A916

  ISBN 0–7451–9129–0

This Large Print edition is published by Chivers Press, England, and
John Curley & Associates, Inc, U.S.A. 1986

Published by arrangement with the author

U.K. Hardback ISBN 0 7451 9129 0
U.S.A. Softback ISBN 0 89340 953 7

He was a black man, Jubal Wills. He was the first ex-slave hired to wear a lawman's badge in a town. A quiet town, Yellowstone City, Montana. Its one hundred citizens elected to hire this man who had made a name for himself in Texas and New Mexico. He packed his belongings and with his wife of eleven months made the long trip by wagon. This was May, 1874.

SCL

CHAPTER ONE

Jubal Wills was the first to see the rider.

That morning in September, Jubal had awakened quickly, thinking he had heard a noise. He lay on his back and did not move, a lank-bodied black man with close-cropped black hair, his long face tight while he listened. He heard no sound except Ellie Mae's slow breathing. Hazy light filtered in along the edges of the window shade, brighter now than a few minutes ago. There was no sound, he was sure of that.

He closed his eyes. After another minute he opened them and stared at the window. The time was still before six, with the sun just coming up. He shifted one foot under the covers. He wiggled his toes of the other to scratch at an itch.

He half-turned to free his too long nightshirt where the cloth had crept up and bunched over his hips. He lay flat and looked at his wife. She was beautiful to him, her soft brown face calm and serene in peaceful sleep. He wanted to touch her, but didn't. She needed her rest. He stared at the white plaster of the ceiling. It was so good to feel, this house. He remembered the rough weathered boards of the plantation shacks, waking to the sounds and smells of that life, and the canvas of the army tents with their odors of sweat and men and gun oil and leather and horseflesh. He wanted to roll over and hold and love as they had so many mornings. They couldn't, not with only a few more weeks to wait.

He could not go back to sleep. And he would wake Ellie Mae if he lay here and moved too much.

He slid out of bed and took his clothes, boots, and gunbelt before he closed the door softly behind him. It was cold for September. He knew the Montana high-plain winters set in early. Not like in Louisiana, Texas, or New Mexico. George Dillon had told them about that. The sheriff had helped so much, even to letting him and Ellie Mae use this house built by the town for the head lawman. Dillon had offered the house, not just because his new deputy had a wife, but also for the baby.

Jubal poured water into the basin. He had been owned as the property of men for the first eighteen years of his life. After Appomattox, freedom was months of wandering, until he heard of the Ninth Cavalry being formed in New Orleans. Eight years he had been a soldier. He had taken orders, and had learned to give orders. He'd met good men and bad. Dillon was the best, making the long ride to seek him out in the hot, dusty plains country above the Rio Grande.

He pulled the nightshirt off over his head. Wearing it was one of the things Ellie Mae had made him change to after their week in Los Carlos. When the baby came, and the three of them were settled, he'd speak to her about that, at least to have her shorten the length so he wouldn't get tangled up every night.

He sighed. She would argue and talk of 'civilizing' him, but he'd make her look back to the Los Carlos week and she'd laugh. He lathered his shoulders and chest with a bar of lye-and-fat soap, and scrubbed the ugly purplish scar that puckered the skin under his right rib casing. It would ache in winter, this reminder of a Comanche lance. He had to live with it and accept it, for it was part of the past. Life was good here in Yellowstone City.

He piled wood in the stove and got a fire going while he put on his clothes. The kitchen would be warm when Ellie Mae woke.

He looked at the bedroom door. He did not hear a sound. She would open her eyes and reach for him and know he was out, and that she was safe. He had always wanted this feeling. He did not buckle on the gunbelt. He'd just have to unbuckle and hang it on one of the office pegs. He held the holstered

3

sixgun in his hand, opened the door, and went outside.

★   ★   ★

Jubal saw the rider then, far out on the grassy flat, coming fast toward the town.

He squinted against the clean yellow shine. He had always liked the brightness of this land. From the first day. Their wagon had been long on the foothills trail between thick walls of dark timber, and they had broken suddenly into the open and a world of endless blue sky and diamond-sparkle sunshine, with the entire upper Calligan Valley stretched wide and green before them.

This morning the sky was as brassy blue as that first day. The ever-present wind seemed to shift and spread the traces of cloud above the distant peaks of the Madison and Gallatin Mountains. It would be a good day.

The rider was Billy Pruitt. Turning out of Cross Street into Grant, Jubal could see how the boy drove his horse. He must have started long before daybreak to cover the six miles from his family's ranch. Billy raised an arm and waved, and then waved again while Jubal passed the blacksmith's, the lumber yard, land office, the restaurant, Myron Stone's general store, and the Shiloh Hotel and the

Drovers Saloon facing each other across the width of the street. No one else was out. Three columns of smoke rose from chimneys in the bigger two-story homes of the town merchants at Grant's west end, showing someone was getting breakfast.

Jubal stepped onto the boardwalk, his tall shadow thrown squat and flat against the front door of the jail.

George Dillon slept on the bunk of the closest cell in the office that smelled strongly of lamp oil and Bull Durham tobacco. Jubal left the door open and moved past the rolltop desk to hang the holster and gunbelt on the rack. Dillon stood. He yawned and rubbed his stubbled jaw. 'You're real early today, Jubal.'

'I thought you could eat before you made the first round,' Jubal said. 'The Pruitt boy is out there riding in.'

'So early?' The sheriff bent to draw on his boots. He was a short, mustached man in his late fifties, with a harsh leanness to his body. He took his tarnished star from the desktop, pinned it on, and went to the door.

The drum of hoofbeats was loud along the west end. Across Grant, Myron Stone and his clerk had come out to lower the store's red and white striped awning. Dillon breathed in deeply. He smelled the wood smoke and the sharp dampish odor of tar weed that drifted down from the high slopes behind the town.

'Billy never goes anyplace slow,' he said. 'Never knew him to.'

'I'll talk to him, Mr. Dillon, if you want to go across.'

Dillon shook his head, watching the boy pull in at the hitchrail. Billy did not tie his gelding. He swung out of the saddle and let the reins hang. He was as tired and sweating as his mount.

'Sheriff!' the boy called. 'We need you out to our place! We've lost cattle and there's...'

'Hold it, boy. Don't rush.' The lawman stepped back to allow Billy inside. 'Slow down now.'

The boy went on talking while he wiped at his forehead and brushed his hand through his thick brown hair.

'We're missin' ten head, Sheriff! There's bound to be tracks where they were!' He stared wide-eyed at Dillon. 'You heard the talk about the Crows actin' up!'

Dillon said, 'The Crows are still in Canada, Billy.'

'But the Army's sendin' more troops out! And General Custer's takin' over at Fort Abe Lincoln for some reason!'

'That's just talk,' Dillon told him. 'There's no reason to worry, not like this.'

6

Billy's hand once more brushed at his hair, his thin face serious. 'Look, Mr. Dillon. Ma's alone with the girls. They're scared. I wouldn't've ridden all this way if we weren't scared. Can you come out and tell them?'

Dillon stared through the open doorway. Myron Stone had gone into his store. His clerk sprinkled water from a can to hold down the dust on the porch and steps. A block west, the Montana-Dakotas Stage Line barn doors were open. Lew Halstead, the hostler, led out the Concord coach team to hitch up for the morning run to Helena. The sheriff's eyes flicked towards the residential section. Smoke showed from more chimneys. Other storekeepers would be out soon, then the people.

Jubal said, 'I'll ride with Billy, Mr. Dillon. I'll put his mother and sisters at ease.'

'Yes,' the sheriff answered. He watched the boy. 'Mr. Wills'll go out and settle them. And you help.' He moved toward the desk. 'You have to hold on better than this, Bill. You're the man out there since your pa died. They're dependin' on you.'

The fourteen-year-old shifted from one boot to the other. 'She wants you, Mr. Dillon.' He would not look at the deputy. 'Ma said you were to come.'

Dillon halted behind the desk. 'Bill, your

7

father wouldn't go off like this. You know he wouldn't. You're in his place.'

The boy's eyes switched from Dillon to the street. He shook his head. 'Ma wants you, Sheriff. She needs you.'

George Dillon exhaled, exasperated. 'All right.' He pulled open the lower drawer and took his holstered Colt and gun-belt. I'll get my horse.'

Jubal said, 'I'll bring him across. You can grab a quick bite.'

'No. If they're that upset, the sooner I reach them the better.'

Billy Pruitt scuffed his boots again. He rubbed both of his hands together and looked away from the sheriff and the deputy. Watching him, Dillin could see the boy was still too tense. Dillon buckled on the gunbelt and adjusted the hang of the holster.

'You make the rounds,' he told Jubal. His voice was calm, quiet. 'Billy, get some water while I'm saddling up. We start now, we'll reach there in time for your ma to give me breakfast.'

*   *   *

Billy rode as hard as he had coming in, keeping his horse always ahead of Dillon's black. The sheriff was irritated at the boy for the way he had acted toward Jubal Wills. Not accepting him as deputy and not wanting to look him in the eyes. It was the wrong treatment to give Jubal, who had done a fine job since he put on a badge. Dillon wondered how Jubal felt about the boy, and the town. Yellowstone County had needed a deputy. One of the Council had heard of a sergeant in the Negro Ninth Cavalry. The people were told of the battle near Fort Davis, and of Apache Pass in New Mexico. And that a Sergeant Wills who had been mentioned in both fights was leaving the Army to get married. The Council voted to hire him. The pay had been little, but it had been the chance for Jubal and Ellie Mae Wills.

Billy had looked through Jubal as if he weren't there. He had been too excited and demanding. Dillon would settle the fear of the boy's mother and sisters. He would talk to Billy about his taking his father's place, and of how to treat a man.

Dillon saw no signs of trouble at the ranches they passed. Cattle grazed contentedly in the meadows close to the homes and barns. Men worked in the yards and about the buildings and fields. Mal Weaver cut timber along the Calligan's high north bank. He stopped his work and waved. Dillon returned the wave, feeling the peace of the people and land,

9

seeing the quiet of the unbroken miles of wide-open range that stretched greenish-brown to the southern rim of the valley. His gaze moved north, following the lazy sweep of the river behind the stand of timber that blocked a view of the Pruitt ranch. What he had thought were clouds above the mountains was actually smoke, hazy and piling up in the distance. Whatever burned—trees, grass— was beyond the sheltering windbreaks of the snowy Madison and Gallatin peaks. He didn't worry about that.

Billy Pruitt slowed at the turnoff. The roof of the log house beyond a copse of aspens and cottonwoods shone gray-white under the sun. Billy motioned past the pole corrals.

'The cattle were out there,' he said. 'I heard some noise, and when I got dressed they were gone.'

'We'll have a look. You and I will ride out.'

'We better see Ma first,' the boy answered. 'You gotta see her first.'

'I will. I know why she's worried.'

'She is. She is. She said for me to bring you straight in.' The house and barn doors were closed, the yard quiet. Billy pointed to the front door. 'Ma's kept the girls inside. She wouldn't let them run to meet us.'

Dillon studied the boy. He was too nervous, just like he had been inside the jail. 'Billy, none of you found Indian signs?'

'No. No, Sheriff, but they're mighty scared.' He held the gelding to allow Dillon's black to go ahead. 'That's why they don't dare even look out. Ma said she wouldn't open for anyone but you.' He rose in the stirrups and called, 'Ma, it's us, me and Mr. Dillon. We're comin' in.'

Dillon did not shift his eyes from the boy. His right hand brushed the stock of his Winchester booted under his knee. He would not draw the carbine, he decided. The two girls were eight and ten years old, and they and their mother were already frightened enough.

'I'll talk to them,' he said. 'Act as though you know there's no threat, Billy. You start now.'

He climbed down and motioned for the boy to go first and open the door.

Billy led through the small entry hallway. Dillon, a step behind, caught sight of Alice Pruitt and her daughters, the three sitting on the cowhide divan. The two small girls, so close to their mother, the woman erect with her hands together in her lap, made Dillon think of a family picture being taken. Told to stay in one spot without motion... The realization came then. He stiffened, aware that the three sets of eyes widened, hearing

11

Billy begin to say, 'Don't, Mr. Dillon...'

The man he saw was tall and thin, a sixgun in his hand. Dillon's right arm swung and hit the hand down, his left was a fist smashing at the man's whiskered face. He felt the impact, heard the man's gasp, and the scrape of noise behind him.

There was no time to draw his gun, only an instant to pivot and catch sight of a big black man and the blur of a rifle barrel that crashed down onto his head. Dillon staggered under the blow, the woman's and girls' screams alive in his mind while the huge man struck again.

Dillon's head, hatless, split and spurted blood as he fell. Swearing, the tall man, a trickle of red widening from his mouth onto his whiskered jaw, lowered his gun's barrel toward Dillon's chest.

Alice Pruitt was on her feet. 'Stop! Don't!' she screamed. 'You wanted the sheriff out here! We did what you wanted!'

Billy reached to grab for the weapon, but the man shoved him away. 'No,' Billy pleaded. 'I got him for you! You said to bring only him and I did!'

'We didn't make a sound,' his mother added. 'Please, don't shoot him! Please!'

'He hit me! No damn lawman tries hittin' me!'

'Don't you shoot, Farnley!' The words were

loud-spoken, an order from the man who came through the front doorway. He was middle-aged and tall with a gray grizzled beard, and he was dressed in faded waist overalls and a patched hickory shirt. He made no move to touch his ancient Colt pistol that hung in a weather-stained holster. 'All's we need is to have somebody hear a gunshot from inside here.'

'He hit me, Paw.' The leveled barrel did not waver. 'I don't let that go.'

Billy waited, poised to try to grab again. Linda Pruitt was crying on the divan, her older sister holding her close and tight. The gray-bearded man glanced at them, then from their mother to Billy. He nodded to the huge man and Farnley. 'You'll git your chance, boy. There's time.'

He stepped between Farnley and the unconscious Dillon, as though he meant to take the sixgun. The instant he was near Billy his right hand lashed out. Alice Pruitt gasped, the girls were shocked into silence when the fist smashed Billy's head and drove him reeling against the wall.

Billy's mother raised her hands to help. The man threw her aside and seized her son's shoulder.

'That's nothin' to what you'll git,' he snarled at the boy. 'Now git out and bring

13

your buckboard around.' His black eyes flashed to the Pruitt women. 'Do like we tell you. Exactly, or everyone of you'll be finished 'fore we go into that town. Move, boy, for that wagon I hitched.'

Billy hurried outside. The bearded man was suddenly calm, his voice quiet. 'We'll drop them off,' he said to Farnley and the huge man. 'Won't be no one to stand against us and Grandpa Andrew. No one to stop us in that town now.'

CHAPTER TWO

Jubal Wills stepped from the sheriff's office into the afternoon sun. He stood on the boardwalk and stared westward. Three men riding alongside a buggy that headed into the town were all he could see beyond the buildings, with no sign of George Dillon.

Jubal had expected the sheriff back hours ago. If he had struck trouble, Jubal thought, he would have sent Billy Pruitt or someone else in for help. He had made the rounds just as Dillon would have made them. He had put off eating until now, after three o'clock. And even now he hesitated before he closed and locked the office.

The clouds which had rolled up over the peaks had worked out toward the high cliffs that closed in the north side of the valley. The temperature had dropped as the damp, smoke-smelling wind blew down off the mountains. Dillon knew a storm would hit; he could be following tracks as far as possible until rain washed them out. That's what the sheriff would do, Jubal believed, what would keep him away so long.

He locked the door. He stood at the edge of the walk. The sun would be below the southern rim in little longer than three hours. Thick shadows stretched across Grant. Thunder made a dull rumble behind the peaks. That's what Sheriff Dillon was doing, Jubal was sure. He was making certain everything was right at the Pruitts'.

He crossed the street. Sunlight flashed from the metal on the delivery wagon tied at Stone's hitchrail. The same whitish glare reflected in the saloon windows, giving a sharp silhouette to the cowhand who stood smoking outside the batwings. A stranger, redheaded with a reddish stubble. Strangers were becoming more and more common, even during the three months Jubal had been in Yellowstone City. A few were drifters, most were from new families which took up homesteads, and some of the larger spreads hired on extra hands to gather and brand the increase in cattle.

Two women talked on the hotel porch. They smiled, and the deputy touched his hatbrim. Mario LoGuidice waved from his barbershop. Lew Halstead spoke to him when he passed the stage company's work area.

Jubal liked this, being noticed and spoken to, and being sure the people meant it. Just like George Dillon had said: when the people are aware a lawman is out, they feel safe. Because of him. He had felt some of this when his troop had patrolled a frontier area and settlers came out of their soddies or shacks to them. The Comanches and Apaches had made that welcome. Yet, even then there were those who showed other feelings to the black cavalry. He had felt it. He had sensed an attitude from Billy Pruitt this morning, the boy's talking not to him but directly to Dillon.

He hadn't found that attitude here, for either himself or Ellie Mae. They'd come north to get away from that, for themselves and the baby, and for the life they would have. Snow closed in the valley almost half the year, and people grew to know each other. That and the security of close, good friends was what he had looked for and found.

Jubal did not turn toward Cross Street. He stopped. The black-topped buggy had reached upper Grant. The driver balanced a rifle across his knees. The man on the seat alongside him held a carbine, and the stocks of weapons jutted from the leather boots of the three horsemen.

The driver, white-haired and white-bearded, watched every stride of Jubal's walk toward them. He spoke quick words out of the corner of his mouth to the tall, gray, grizzled-bearded man alongside him. He drew up his bony horse. Neither man made a motion to shift the weapons that rested across their laps.

Jubal halted at the step plate. 'Didn't you see the sign at the town limits?' he asked. 'We have a no-gun law here.'

The driver was older than he had seemed at a distance, short and narrow and round-shouldered, his white hair silky. His hollow-cheeked face stared down at the deputy badge. Two deep lines at the edges of his thin mouth showed smudges of chewing tobacco while he spoke.

'We're jest passin' through,' he offered in a slow drawl. 'We want to eat a bite, and we'll push on.'

'You'll have to put up those guns. No guns are to be carried in this town.'

'How 'bout keepin' them in a boot?' the second man said. He was twenty years younger than the driver, wearing faded waist overalls and a patched hickory shirt. He

17

glanced at the three riders calmly, and as calmly he squinted to study what he could see along Grant. 'Grandpa here needs food and rest. We hear there's Crows out. Don't want to git caught without a firearm.'

'The Crows aren't causing any trouble,' Jubal told them. 'The Indians you'll strike in this territory are friendly.'

'Wal, we hear the Army's movin' more cavalry into Fort Abe Lincoln,' the younger one began.

The driver did not let him finish. He swung around and reached behind them to take a scarred leather saddle scabbard from the rear seat. 'We'll leave them booted. Both our pieces. That all right with you?' His tone sharpened. 'Yours too, Longstreet. Shuck it.' He nodded at Jubal and slid the rifle's iron barrel in. 'We'll leave them in back, Deputy. That all right?'

'Long as it's in the boot,' Jubal answered, watching the other man reach around and pick up a second leather scabbard. He jammed his weapon in and laid it on the floor. The three riders, young men in their late teens and early twenties, held their reins clear of the carbine stocks.

Jubal motioned toward the Dutchman's. 'You'll get food in the restaurant. The hotel has a kitchen for roomers.'

'Obliged,' the driver said, and he jiggled the lines.

Jubal watched the buggy and horsemen. There was something he did not like about the gray-bearded one. A feeling, a tightness, like the tension of a wire drawn too snug. The law was written that way: rifles and carbines were allowed if they were kept booted. With the mountain lions and rattlers, and lately the talk about the Crows, the ranchers and farmers had to have protection when they were away from their homes. The buggy turned in toward the restaurant, and Jubal walked on.

He caught sight of Ellie Mae when he was still three houses from his own. She waited in the front parlor window, the curtain pulled open so she could look out and watch for him. She dropped the curtain into place, stepped to the hallway door, and opened it as he came up the steps.

The good smells of cooked chicken and baking pies were strong in the house, and he knew she had kept a hot fire that would hold off a storm's coldness. The house felt warm and comfortable and safe.

He could see the table was set and waiting through the kitchen doorway. Ellie Mae had changed the front room into a sewing center. White cloth cut for diapers, pins, needles, thimbles, scissors, and tiny patterns lay

19

spread over the furniture. She smiled at him and lifted her cheek for his kiss. Then she took a pair of tiny pink booties from atop the table.

'These are for a girl,' she said. She rumpled through the pile and brought out a blue copy of the booties. 'And these if she's a boy.'

'If she's a boy!' He laughed and wrapped both arms around her to hug her. She moved the bulge of her stomach away and laughed. 'Your belt and gun, Jubal.'

He unbuckled the gunbelt and draped it over a chair. She hurried into the kitchen, still smiling. He followed her.

'Can't stay long,' he told her. 'Mr. Dillon went out to one of the ranches early this morning.'

'You have to eat, Jubal. You've been left alone before and had time for your meals.'

'The Pruitts had some cows missing. Mr. Dillon went out to check. Billy Pruitt came in with more of that talk about the Crows.' He sat, and Ellie Mae set a plate of chicken in front of him. She returned to the stove. He added, 'I might have to stay all night. But I'll look in on you.'

'You stay at your work.' She brought a bowl of potatoes and hot biscuits and put them on the table. 'I have to be used to my man staying at his work.'

'I'll look in.'

'You'll do your work. Eat now.' She turned to the stove again and spooned carrots into a bowl. Jubal did not start his meal. He watched his wife, feeling the easy quiet and warmth of the high-ceilinged, immaculate kitchen, and a softness made by the white curtains. He'd been so lucky to find Ellie Mae in a town like San Antonio. She had made such a change in his life, not wanting to follow the Army camps. Together they'd decided on taking the deputy's job. He was continually amazed that this beautiful, so dark-haired and fine-bodied woman would be the mother of his children . . .

The noise of a shot killed the thought. The bang of a gun sounded so far off he believed it had come from out on the flat. It was followed by two more rapid, louder blasts.

He was on his feet, aware of his gunless hips. He ran through the kitchen doorway and into the parlor, hearing his wife's steps behind him.

'Lock the door,' he ordered as he grabbed the gunbelt. 'Stay inside here.'

Outside he broke into a run. Yells came from the center and backside of the town. Jubal whipped the cartridge belt around his waist, but he moved so fast he could not grasp and hook the buckle.

21

He ran on. He did not slow, holding the belt and holster in his left hand and the drawn .44 Colt in his right, angry at himself for being careless enough to take off the weapon in the first place, so unthinking and careless he could end up paying as a lawman for it.

CHAPTER THREE

Men had poured out of the close homes. Women and children had appeared in their doorways and windows. Fred Ashwood, who owned the livery, was already on his side lawn, his two lanky sons with him. They were talking and staring toward the rear of the general store.

'Sounded like it was over there!' Ashwood called to Jubal. 'Inside the store!'

'Go back in your house.' The deputy shifted his run to pass them. 'The sheriff's out of town. Keep your wives and kids in.'

'Dillon's away?' Ashwood asked. He swung around to his sons as Jubal went through their back yard.

Most of the people had stayed on their porches or in their yards, watchful and silent, the chatter that did go on among them held down. A man and a small boy were behind

Stone's store. Jubal believed they had rushed outside to watch. Then the man stumbled. The coat of his dark suit flapped open, and Jubal could see blood on his shirtfront. The boy grabbed the man's shoulder and tried to keep him on his feet. But the man slumped to the ground.

Wagon wheels jounced and creaked in the store alleyway. Jubal passed the store's small barn and stone well and reached the downed man and the boy just as the store's rear door was flung open. The gray-whiskered man wearing overalls and a hickory shirt charged out holding a rifle. The wounded man tried to push to his feet. He did not have the strength, and fell onto his side.

The black-topped buggy rolled noisily out of the alley. Its white-haired, white-bearded driver, whip in hand, slashed at the horse. The three young riders followed on their mounts and pulled in alongside the driver.

'Drop that rifle!' Jubal shouted the order. The click of his Colt's hammer cocking snapped loud in the silence.

'Keep out of this, Deputy!' the driver called. 'Finish him, Longstreet! Get on with it!' He had the buggy stopped, and he bent to grab his own weapon from the floorboards.

The whiskered features of Longstreet did not change as he took a step forward. 'Git,

Deputy,' he said tightly. 'This ain't none of your business.'

The fallen man raised an arm, and the boy tried to help him. Tears streamed down the boy's small, terrified face. 'They want to kill us!' he pleaded. 'Both of us! Don't let them!'

Myron Stone's round figure pushed past the store's rear door. 'That man isn't armed,' he said to Jubal. 'He was shot without a chance.'

Jubal's stare stayed on the man with the rifle, his Colt barrel held centered on his chest. 'Drop it. Now. Old Man, don't pull that from its boot.'

'Throw down on him, Grandpaw!' one of the riders cried. 'He cain't git five of us.'

'Drop the rifle like the deputy says!' Fred Ashwood's voice was high-pitched, tense. The livery owner stepped in behind Jubal. He had a Remington revolver in his hand. His two sons held Winchester carbines, pumped and leveled at Longstreet and the old man and the riders.

Jubal took the rifle from Longstreet and gave it to Ashwood. He pulled the sheathed weapon from the driver's hands. The old man sat motionless, his eyes on the boy and his wounded father.

'Owen McClain,' he said. 'You run this far. You'll run no farther.'

McClain did not answer. He had succeeded

24

in sitting, doubled over, one hand tight against his left shoulder to control the blood. His face was pasty white, making him look as old as the buggy's driver. 'Go inside, Peter,' he told the boy. 'Go 'head.'

'Pa, I want to stay with you. Pa!'

Jubal motioned to Longstreet with the Colt. 'Over to the jail.' The tall, gray-whiskered man would not move. He simply glared hatefully down at McClain. 'You won't keep your luck. Not now with my family knowin' where you are.'

Myron Stone stared at Longstreet and shook his head. 'I couldn't believe it. They were standing at my dry goods counter when he came in. He started shooting the minute he saw them.'

Jubal looked at Fred Ashwood. 'Take him over to the jail. You and your boys.'

'You got no right lockin' him up,' the white-haired driver said. The three on horseback edged in closer, their hands near their carbine stocks. 'The McClains killed half our kin. They did, Deputy. Longstreet was evenin' up.'

'Owen McClain killed my brother,' Longstreet said, pointing. 'Ten years ago, he did. I been after him, Deputy. You got no call stoppin' this.'

Jubal looked at the wounded man, sitting

25

stiff and glassy-eyed. Then at the boy. 'Where are you from?'

Longstreet answered for McClain. 'Missouri. Coleson County. He was there with his kin. They killed enough of us Trollers. They . . .'

'You brought a family feud all this distance? You came here like this after a boy?'

'He's a McClain. We tracked them.'

Jubal motioned again to Fred Ashwood. 'Take him to the jail.' The white-haired driver cursed and began to sputter. 'Quiet down,' Jubal went on. 'You sent him to start shooting in the middle of this town. You turn that horse and move out of here.'

The driver picked up the reins. 'Don't you worry, Longstreet,' he said. 'You won't be held long.' He eyed the young riders, who watched Myron Stone help McClain to his feet. 'You settin' bail, Deputy?'

'No bail. Not until the circuit judge comes. You want to argue, wait for the sheriff.'

The old man's face turned toward the Ashwoods as they led Longstreet into the alleyway. The deep lines on either side of his bearded mouth twitched until he bit down on his lip. He spat a blob of tobacco juice between his feet.

'You got no right interferin'. No right atall, boy.' He pulled the horse to the left. The crowd, mostly men but with a few women and children at the rear, opened a broad path for the wagon to roll toward Cross Street.

Myron Stone had McClain's black coat open so he could see the wound. Blood seeped through the fingers tightened over the shoulder, the red blotch spreading down the man's chest. Doctor John Hobson, a long, gangling man dressed in a conservative brown suit and spotless shirt and collar, came through the crowd. 'Don't move the arm,' he said to McClain. And to Jubal, 'I'll take him over to my office.'

'We'll have to talk to him.'

'He won't be going far until he's patched.' He braced the wounded side and started McClain from the yard. The boy, his face streaked with tears and dust, trailed along after them.

Myron Stone said, 'I never saw anything like it. Longstreet came past the screen door shooting. He knew they were inside. If Mr. McClain didn't pull the boy behind the counter, both of them would be dead.'

'McClain wasn't trying to buy one of those new Winchesters you have in the display case?'

'No, Jubal. They only wanted to rent the upstairs spare room. Said he couldn't afford the hotel more than one night. He wants to settle in this town.'

An outbreak of low talk, punctuated here and there by a harsh grumble, traveled through the onlookers. Jubal studied the people, noting how they bunched close to hear. Those at the rear asked what had been said. Myron's statement spread to the listeners, and they did not like it any better than the men and women at the front.

'I'll be in later,' Jubal told the storekeeper. He paused a moment and made certain the buggy and three riders were beyond the last of the buildings. Then he started along the alleyway.

*　　　*　　　*

'He's goin' to the jail,' Farnley Troller said. He had turned his tall body in the saddle to look back. 'We should've shot up their town and got Paw loose 'fore they had a chance to think.'

'We could've,' his cousin Calem Troller agreed. He had the long, bony face of the family, his anger quick like Farnley's. 'I say we go back and take him.'

'Black bastard,' said Ulysses Troller, his brother. 'I don't cotton to leavin' just 'cause he hid behind that badge. I want a chance at him.'

'You'll git it,' Grandpa Andrew told them, glad the boys were riled and on edge like this. They'd act when they had to, and he had the way. He did not feel they had lost one thing in having Longstreet˙ locked up. They knew where Owen McClain was, and his son. If that deputy thought he could talk down to them and hold a Troller in a cell for a judge to put a noose around his neck, he had plenty to learn. He kept the buggy moving at a slow roll. He rubbed at an itch in his beard while he looked across his shoulder.

The men, women, and children had split their crowd and all fanned out toward their houses. Smart, dang them, smart to get clear of the line of fire. He couldn't have moved, couldn't have tried, with four guns on Longstreet and himself and the boys. But there'd danged-sight be a good bit of shooting if the town didn't see fit to let Longstreet go. They had no worry about the McClains. They were cornered, with no way out of the valley. They'd get both of them easy enough.

'Grandpaw,' Calem said, 'there's Bean.'

'You want me to cut down the sonovabitch?' Farnley said. 'I'll do it.'

The slight movement of the old man's hand quieted them. The buggy wheels rumbled noisily over the thick planks of the river bridge. Ahead, where the clustered willows, cottonwoods, and alders opened, the rider waited. He was a short redhead with a freckled face and a reddish stubble of beard. In the three months Andrew Troller had known Bean, he'd seen only a cold, careful stare on the man's face. The stare was there now, and also a question.

'You missed them?' Bean said flatly. 'And you lost Longstreet, too?'

'We didn't miss,' Farnley snapped. 'You told us they was in the rest'rant. They weren't, and Paw run across by himself soon's he spotted them in the store.'

'They were eatin'. I told you right. They come in on the stage last night and took a hotel room. They were in eatin' when I rode out.'

'No, you bastard,' Farnley spat. 'You got my paw took.'

Bean's red head shook. 'We found them for you,' he said. He swung his mount away from Farnley and Calem, who were edging their horses closer. He looked at the old man. 'Me and Joe Jack were told one hundred dollars.'

Andrew Troller draped the reins across one knee. 'When we finished,' he said. He added when Bean's face tightened, 'That's what we agreed, when we finished. I want you to ride out and send Frank and Clifton in. And we need Joe Jack in here.'

'Mr. Troller, we set up the ranch family and

the sheriff. We tracked the McClains.'

'Joe Jack'll help. He'll do what he's told. You go out and stay for him.'

'Look, Mr. Troller . . .'

'Do it, boy. 'Fore the storm hits, or I'll turn Farnley loose on you and he'll go out. That Nigra'll have the money all for himself.'

The redhead sat straight in his saddle. Ulysses sidled his mount out, away from Farnley and Calem. Bean was in the center of the triangle facing the old man.

'I'll send Joe,' Bean said. He backed his horse away.

Grandpa Andrew did not watch him. He lifted his face to the sky. Lightning flashed around the distant peaks, yet he knew the storm which had held off all day was still a good hour from coming. The damp wind that blew down off the high slopes was sharp with the tangy, pungent smell of washed pine and sage. Just like at home, the smell, the feel of the breeze alive and cold on his face. They'd be through here and heading home soon, to claim what was theirs, what always had been theirs.

'That buck'll earn his money,' he said. 'He goes after the deputy, it'll just be one black after another. Won't be no problem then, to go in and get Longstreet out and finish the McClains.'

CHAPTER FOUR

Jubal turned the key in the cell door. Longstreet Troller swore from behind the iron bars. 'You got no right lockin' me up, Deputy.'

Jubal moved out of the cell block corridor, and Longstreet shouted after him. 'You got no right. You'll pay. Your town'll pay.'

Fred Ashwood and his sons waited at the desk. 'We'll stay and help until the sheriff comes back,' the father told Jubal. 'Dave can ride out to Pruitt's and tell what's happened.'

'I don't want you away from town,' Jubal said. 'That family's out there, and they know you.'

'You'll need some help,' Dave Ashwood said. 'Tom and I'll stay.'

Jubal stood thoughtfully. For a moment his eyes stayed on the flat planes of Dave's dark-burned face and his blond hair parted deep on the side. 'If you'll stay inside, it's enough.' He looked at the father. 'You and Tom should be home, in case that gang comes back.'

Fred Ashwood opened his mouth to answer, but at the sound of footsteps on the walk beyond the doorway he turned. Two members of the Town Council came in.

Oakley Hall, the mayor, was Yellowstone City's blacksmith. Bull-necked and thick-chested, he looked worried. Harold Shanks, the banker, was a sanguine, hearty man with a large balding head and jowls that shook when he laughed. There wasn't a trace of a smile on his face now.

'Do you expect George Dillon will be back soon?' Hall asked. He glanced past Jubal at the cell block. 'He should be told.'

'I'll have someone go out, Mayor,' Jubal said.

'Hey,' Longstreet Troller called. 'You're the mayor, you can make him let me go. You got no call holdin' me.'

Hall looked away from the shout and would not answer.

'My kin'll come back. You c'n damn-well decide on that. You want that for your town? You c'n damn-well count on it!'

'You think they will be back?' Shanks said. He stared through the window into the street. It was exactly what Jubal knew it would be like after trouble. People had drifted out into Grant. They stood in twos and threes and small groups near the hotel and on the general store porch and steps, and in the shade of the alleyways. Boys were among them, jumping up and down or pushed onto their tiptoes to see inside the jail office.

33

'I figure they will,' Jubal said. 'Dave is going to stay with the prisoner while I talk to McClain.'

'I can stay,' Hall offered. 'Harold and I.'

'You'd do better to move that crowd, Mr. Hall. Get them clear of the office. We don't know what'll happen.'

'Yes,' Shanks agreed. 'They'll break up if we ask them to, Oakley.'

Hall nodded and turned toward the door. Then, as quickly, he swung about and faced Jubal. 'You'll send for George Dillon.'

'As soon as I can, Mr. Hall.' Jubal paused while the Council members left with Fred and Tom Ashwood. 'Lock the door from the inside,' he told Dave. He stepped onto the walk and pulled the door shut behind him.

*   *   *

He felt the sun on his shoulders and chest. When he'd gone home to eat, he hadn't noticed the warmth. Now, despite the sun being low in the southwest and the clouds to the north, he felt a sticky sweat across his back and under his arms, and he was very much aware of the heat and of how the wide shadows of the false-fronted buildings stretched beyond mid-street. The heat had always affected him once he was tight or strained, in

34

the days he had picked cotton in the fields, or trained horses, or gone out on patrol with the cavalry troop when the hostiles were near. He could no more stop it than he could stop the Trollers from keeping after the McClains. No more than he could stop them from being somewhere near the town.

Doctor Hobson's waiting room was small and bare except for six straight-backed chairs lined along one wall. Through the inner office door Jubal could see the doctor, glasses on, bent over McClain atop the high wooden surgical table. The doctor did not glance around. He kept his attention on his patient. His thin fingers moved deftly, capably, while he cleaned the wound with hot water and carbolic acid. McClain's son, his face dust-streaked and red around the eyes, waited in a chair beside the glass medical cabinet.

Jubal stopped near the boy. McClain's eyes were open. He watched his son, and the deputy. He said softly, 'I don't want him hurt. He's only seven. He isn't part of the feud.'

'Quiet,' the doctor ordered. 'Don't move. I'll lose the pieces of cloth.'

A hush came and lasted a half hour, broken only by the movements of the doctor and a low gasp when the wounded man drew in his breath. Finally, the doctor straightened and stared at McClain over his steel-rimmed glasses. 'You were lucky the bullet went clean through. Another quarter inch and it would have splintered the collar bone. I think I have all the shreds of cloth out of there, but I want to see you in the morning to make certain.'

'I'll be in, Doctor. Thank you.' McClain began to sit. He was too weak and had to drop back onto the pillow.

'You lost a lot of blood,' the doctor told him. His long-boned, serious face turned to Jubal. 'He'll need a place to rest. And for the boy. It'll have to be a safe spot for days. Maybe a week.'

'We have room in the jail. No one will get to him.'

McClain spoke quickly. 'Not the jail.' His tone calmed. He shook his head. 'Not for my son. Longstreet Troller is in there. It isn't the place for Peter.'

Jubal knew McClain was right. He gazed about the office, and at the doctor near the sink cleaning the bloody water from the basin. McClain said, 'We'll have the room over the store. We'll be all right.'

'I'm not sure,' said Jubal.

'We will, Deputy.' Slowly the wounded man pushed himself erect with his good arm. 'We won't go out of the room. We'll leave as soon as I'm in shape.' He took his red-stained shirt frm a chair and began to slip it across his shoulders. 'Your people have no part in our trouble. Or your town. We'll leave.'

Jubal said, 'Mr McClain, I don't understand a feud. So much hate between people. I don't understand.'

'I don't either,' answered McClain. He eyed his son, as though he spoke directly to him. 'I grew up in the feud. I thought I understood when I was younger, but when Peter was born . . . His mother died then. She was from out of our county. She made me promise.' His head shook. 'I thought we'd gotten away from it for good. But we didn't.'

'They've been hunting you for seven years. You don't even have a gun.'

'I don't want one. I was part of it as a boy. I shot two Trollers, like Longstreet says. But it was before Jennie and Peter.' His eyes flickered from the boy to Jubal. 'You know what started it, Deputy? Twenty-two years ago? Before the war? Land. My grandfather homesteaded some farm land the county gave him, and the Trollers claimed ownership because they had planted as far as our river. I was only ten, three years older than Peter. After my grandfather was shot and killed, I was given a gun, and started Troller-hunting with my family.' His voice fell off in his effort to stand. Jubal held his arm for support. 'That life isn't for my son. St. Louis, Abilene,

37

Virginia City. We've shifted from one place to another. I thought we were safe.'

'You are safe,' Jubal said, 'both of you.' He moved with the man and his son toward the waiting room. 'I'll come over with him in the morning, Doc.'

Hobson lifted his glasses off his nose, watching the boy. 'Stay in your room. Both of you, Mr. McClain. I'll stop in to see you.'

'We will. Thank you, Doctor.'

'Thank you,' Peter echoed. He walked ahead of his father and Jubal to the outside door. His small hand gripped the knob.

'I'll open and see it's safe,' Jubal told him. He waved the boy back alongside his father. 'Wait until I make sure.'

★   ★   ★

There wasn't a sign of the Trollers. The day was darker, chillier. Jubal crossed Grant with the McClains. He could see Myron Stone waiting inside the screen door of his store.

The heavy-set storekeeper and his Mexican clerk both held blankets. 'Ramon's made up your beds,' he told McClain. 'We're putting these extras in the room. It gets cold nights.'

'That's fine, Mr. Stone.' McClain moved his head from side to side, but not in disagreement or doubt. 'I don't know how to tell you. You've been very fine.' His eyes switched from Stone to Jubal. 'All of you.'

'I have a shirt for you,' Myron told him. 'you won't need a thing.' He rested one hand on Peter's shoulder. 'You can help us clean up our storeroom.' He saw Ramon's dark head nod. The clerk was in his early twenties, slender, with black wavy hair. He led along the aisle between the counters.

'I'll look in,' Jubal said. 'Mr. Dillon will, when he comes back.'

McClain stared around. 'We appreciate this, Deputy, everything you've done.' When Jubal nodded, he continued on with his son.

'Myron,' Jubal said. The storekeeper slowed. 'Be sure the storeroom's outside door is always locked. Don't take one chance.'

'I've already locked it. Do you think the old man will be back?'

'He will. With the rest of them. Could I use Ramon to ride out to Pruitt's and tell Mr. Dillon?'

Stone nodded. 'I'll send him right away.'

Jubal walked to the porch screen door. He listened until he heard the door on the second floor open and then close. He stepped outside, unsure of the street, or when or where the Trollers would again appear. His hand was on his Colt's butt.

He heard his name spoken. 'Jubal.'

Ellie Mae waited near the alleyway mouth. Jubal dropped his hand, aware of a terrible sudden fear that coursed through him. 'I told you to stay inside,' he said sharply. 'I meant it.'

She stood with her hands clenched in front of the round bulge of her blue gingham dress. Her dark eyes stared into his. She looked so pretty, with her black hair holding the last rays of the shine of sunlight. 'You didn't eat, Jubal. I've put your meal onto plates to take to your office.'

He said, 'No, I don't want you near the office. I want you safe. Go over to the Lashways' house and stay with them 'til I come home.' He watched the street, both walks, the alleys, the buildings and doorways and windows. 'Sleep there with them.'

'But I want to be here when you come tonight.'

'Stay at the Lashways'. Ramon is going after Mr. Dillon. I won't be home all night.' He moved closer to her and added in a quiet voice, 'I won't be home for a day or so. I want to know you're safe.'

She met his stare, her eyes anxious, fearful. She did not question him. 'I'll be safe,' she answered. She turned and went along the walk toward Cross Street.

*   *   *

David Ashwood watched Ellie Mae Wills turn
into the side street, and how Jubal did not
move while his wife was in sight. Ashwood
had waited at the window, the Winchester
carbine in his hands. He had watched for the
deputy to leave the general store. Jubal Wills
and his wife had been his family's neighbors
since they had come to Yellowstone City. The
Ashwoods liked their quiet, decent ways.
David's mother planned to help after their
baby was born. He, his father, and his brother
had run for their weapons so the deputy
wouldn't have to handle the trouble alone.
He'd seen the worry on Jubal's face out
behind the store. David could read worry
now, in the deputy's slow stride, and in the
way he watched the street while he crossed
toward the office.

'You listen to me,' Longstreet Troller's
voice called from the cell. 'You be smart and
do what I said.'

David did not answer. He had no right to;
he wasn't a deputy, but just filling in. He did
not turn from the window.

'Damn you! Damn you, boy! You got to
feed me! You keep me stuck in here, I want
food!'

David laid the carbine flat on the desk and

41

turned the key in the lock. He closed the door when Jubal stepped inside.

Jubal asked, 'Will you stay until Mr. Dillon gets back? I'll send word down to your house.'

'I will. My brother and Pa will spell me.'

'Just you is enough. You won't be bothered once the trouble's taken from here.' He looked toward the cell block at Longstreet Troller's loud, demanding yell. 'What's goin' on, you two? I said I'm hungry! Deputy, you gotta feed me!'

'His mouth is as big as his hate,' Dave Ashwood said. 'He hasn't stopped his gripin' since you went out.'

Jubal walked into the cell block. Longstreet stood with his body and whiskered face pressed close to the vertical iron bars. His forehead and cheeks were sweaty and shiny in the light that filtered down through the stone wall's single high-barred window.

'Deputy, 'bout time you came in. I told that close-mouth I should be brought food. I do eat, Deputy. I know you got to open up and go across and bring me food.'

'You'll be fed.'

'Wal, that's more like it. I don't cotton to anyone bein' uppity with me.'

Longstreet eased his posture. He wiped his face and rested on one elbow, very confident. His features broke into a grin when Jubal

42

entered the rear cubicle and pulled at the iron chain supporting the cell bunk. 'You ain't gonna chain me, Deputy? I ain't tryin' to git away. I don't have to, with my kin out there.'

'Your kin'll be in there with you. If they try taking you with guns.' He could not loosen the chain. Oakley Hall would have to do it with his tools. He stepped into the corridor and faced Troller. 'When the sheriff gets back, I'll fix it so your people will make no more trouble for this town.'

Troller gripped the bars. 'Look, boy.'

'You shot at a boy, mister. And an unarmed man.'

'That's none of your affair. We told you what it is. That's our land the McClains were usin'. They killed our kin!'

'McClain tried to quit years ago. I don't understand why they just can't live on their land. They tried . . .'

'They tried! That's right, they tried to run and keep runnin'! They got away with it until people who know 'bout our fight saw them in Virginia City!' He gripped the bars tighter, his knuckles bloodless and white. 'They're cornered now! You'll get the same if I'm not let out of here! Boy, you don't know my kin!'

'Jubal, hurry out here, Jubal,' Dave Ashwood called past the iron-barred doors.

Jubal took only one step before loud yells

43

came from outside the jail. 'Longstreet! We're here, Longstreet! You jest hold on, you hear!'

'I hear!' Longstreet shouted. 'Paw, I hear! I told you, Deputy! You don't know my kin! You will! You damned well will!'

Dave Ashwood had backed to the middle of the office, his Winchester held level. He stared fearfully at Jubal. Through the window, the black-topped buggy seemed bigger than it had in the store yard. Grandpa Andrew on the seat and five horsemen turned in a line from the center of the street toward the hitchrail. The two riders Jubal had not seen before wore black suits, and black flat-crowned hats pulled low over their eyes.

Grandpa Andrew had a rifle lying flat across his lap. Each horseman held a carbine ready. The wheels of the wagon and the hoofs of the horses made a rough, arrogant grumble in the dusty roadway.

Jubal reached both of his hands into the gunrack and pulled two double-barreled shotguns from their places. 'Check this,' he said as he handed Dave one weapon. While Dave broke his, Jubal checked his load of No. 10 shells.

'Cover me from the window,' Jubal added. 'Let them see enough of you to know you're in here. If shooting starts, don't open the door. Make what's left of them break in and you can

44

get them with that Greener.'

'You're crazy!' Longstreet began. 'Paw, he's plannin' t'use...'

'Close your mouth,' Jubal ordered, his words bringing a quick silence. 'One word, I'll take that paw of yours first!'

He waited until the wagon and riders were barely feet from the rail. He opened the door and let it slam loudly shut behind him as he stepped outside, the shotgun up and cocked.

Grandpa Andrew Troller's lips cracked to speak.

The motion of Jubal's weapon, the twin barrels centered on the old white-bearded, white-haired man's chest, cut off any talk.

'Stop there. Drop the reins and hand down your guns,' Jubal ordered. 'All of you, I want them now.'

CHAPTER FIVE

The buggy was motionless, the riders stiff and straight in their saddles. The two in black suits edged their mounts toward the side of the hitchrail. Jubal, squinting against the red sun glaring out from behind the southwest peaks, made a quick gesture with the heavy shotgun barrels. 'Right there,' he repeated.

'Don't try to box me in.'

The taller of the pair shot a look at Grandpa Andrew and Farnley Troller. He muttered an obscene curse. 'We c'n ride over him.'

'Hold y' tongue,' Grandpa Andrew snapped. His eyes stared through the office window, his deep-wrinkled features set in a closed, unrevealing expression. Muscles cramped along Jubal's sweaty spine and down his legs. One word, one motion by the old man and they'd open up. He raised the twin muzzles an inch, another, directly into Andrew Troller's face. He watched only Andrew's deliberate manner and narrowed eyes.

'You'll obey the law, all of you,' the deputy said. 'Mister Troller, you decide.'

The old man's stare returned to Jubal. He was very much conscious of the townspeople about the street and walks and porches, everyone who had stopped to listen. Four men pushed past the Drovers Saloon's swinging batwings. They stayed where they were, in a small knot; not one held a gun, a glass, or a bottle in any hand.

'You got no right lockin' our kin in there,' the old man said coldly.

'He shot a man, Mr. Troller. A man without a gun. He tried to kill a boy.'

'They was McClains.'

46

'You'll obey the law too, Mr. Troller. I'll take those weapons, and you can go in and speak to your son.'

The old man allowed a faint smile, but it did not relieve the expression about his eyes. 'Clifton's right. We can ride over you.'

'He might,' Jubal answered. 'Whoever takes these two loads won't. The man inside would chew up at least two more of you before you reach the cell block. Your feud worth that, Mr. Troller?'

Farnley Troller jerked his mount's neck high, the animal close over the deputy's head. 'That buckshot'd be wasted on our horses. Grandpaw, I'll be willin' . . .'

'This is my place,' the grandfather cut in. 'Keep your place while I'm talkin'.'

Farnley silenced. His ugly stare did not shift from Jubal's face, and Jubal knew the man thought of some future time when things would be different. Grandpa Andrew said, 'We ain't fought for twenty-two years to stop now. Not that, boy.' He straightened on the seat and called through the window. 'Longstreet! Hear me, Longstreet!'

'I do, Paw.' The answer was muffled but audible.

'You stick right there, Longstreet. You done nothin' wrong, son. You come after a man who killed your kin. You done nothin'

47

wrong and you'll be let out of there.' He didn't pause for an answer, simply lowered his voice to the others. 'Give him the pieces.' He held out his rifle, carefully, so every watching eye could witness what he did.

'Grandpaw?' Farnley began.

'It's their law. We got ways we'll want them to abide by here. We obey their laws.'

The old man's bearded face was sure. He nodded while Jubal took his weapons. Farnley muttered a curse, then threw his carbine at Jubal's feet. Ulysses Troller, Clifton Troller, and the others threw theirs down beside Farnley's, splattering dust and dirt onto the deputy's boots.

'We obeyed your law,' Andrew Troller said, his words clear of anger and loud enough for all ears to hear. Turning his head from one side to the other, he included the onlookers in the street and alleyways, on the walks and porches. 'We have our own ways. We'll be back.' He raised the reins.

Jubal said, 'You can go inside and talk.'

'I've talked to my son,' the old man told him low and cold. 'He knows I did.'

While the horses backed and the wagon swung, Dave Ashwood stepped out of the office. He stood with the deputy and watched the line of riders go along Grant toward the hotel.

'He's a bad one,' Dave said. 'He doesn't see any wrong.'

Jubal did not answer. Something wasn't right about how the old man had given in, something he did not trust. He bent over and began to collect the weapons.

★   ★   ★

It had gone as he had wanted, Grandpa Andrew Troller thought. Exactly as he wanted. He'd learn, the black boy would. He slowed the buggy before he reached the hotel. He held the reins. 'Clifton, you drive around to the barn,' he said.

Clifton stepped from his horse's saddle and the stirrups onto the wagon seat. He was beardless and smooth-faced at sixteen, the youngest of Longstreet's sons. He was the best at handling horses. 'I'll be in, Grandpaw. I'll have it with me.'

The old man shifted his body to balance himself while he went off the step plate. He felt every strain in his bones and knew this was his last time away from Coleson. He would finish the trouble and finish it right, and boys like Clifton would never again have the trouble or the duty hanging over them. They wouldn't waste time. It was right, this way.

49

'That'll be heavy for Cliff,' said Farnley. 'I c'n help.'

'Inside,' was all his grandfather answered. He waited while the others tied up. The sky darkened, the clouds were almost over the town. Lightning flashes had reached the creek. The following thunder was loud. The storm would help Joe Jack, the old man knew. Wet and mud would slow the people who came out of their homes, the clouds making the night pitch dark. It would be finished by midnight, with Longstreet free and away from the threat of having to stand trial for an act that was a family duty.

The hotel lobby was small and carpetless. A battered leather divan and six cane-backed chairs were the only furnishings. The clerk waited behind the registration desk. He was a bald, bird-like man, his bare head grayish in the flame of the coal-oil lamp strung above the key rack. He wore a clean white shirt, the sleeves rolled to the elbows, and a thick gold watch chain that also reflected the light.

He nodded when the grandfather spoke for the group. 'Four of you will have to double up,' he said. 'Two to a room.'

'We'll take them,' the old man told him. 'Might be a week or so. With our troubles.'

The clerk nodded once more and turned the registration ledger. 'I'll have another room tomorrow, after a harness and leather drummer leaves.'

'That's what we want,' Andrew said. He wrote his name and stood aside to allow the others to sign.

The lobby rear door opened. Clifton Troller came in. He carried a heavy burlap bag slung over his shoulder.

The clerk's gaze ran across the boy. He leaned over the counter, and said when Clifton started toward the second floor stairs, 'You'll have to sign your name. Each of you has to sign.'

'Sure,' the boy answered. He crossed the lobby and set the bag down alongside the desk.

'Watch it!' Farnley warned. He reached out, too late to stop the bag from opening. The clerk had watched the top folds of burlap slip apart. He saw the gunbelts and holstered sixguns the boy had brought in.

'Hey, you're not supposed to . . .' the clerk began. He stepped back as though he had touched something hot and had been burned. His fingers shook while he reached to close the ledger.

'You live in here?' Grandpa Andrew asked him.

'No, out at the west end.' He wiped the hand across his jaw. 'I don't want any

51

trouble.'

'You have a room to stay in when you have to?'

'Yes, but I—I won't say anything. I've got a wife and kids.'

'You'll stay inside 'til we leave,' the old man said. 'One of us'll always be with you.' He reached into the burlap bag and drew out a long-barreled pistol. He revolved the loaded drum, then jammed the weapon under his waistband and buttoned his coat to hide the handle. 'I'll set down here with you just to make sure.'

*   *   *

Andrew Troller was on the hotel porch when the rider entered the town.

Jubal Wills stepped out and moved along the street for the evening round, and he saw when the old man came out onto the porch and sat in a cane-backed chair. Lamps were lit on porches and inside the stores and houses. After Jubal made the turn from the west end toward the residential section, he saw two more Trollers had joined the grandfather to sit and rock. A fine rain was in the air, a mist of drizzle that gave a wet shine to the yellow squares of light which beamed down from the windows and doorways.

Jubal did not trust the old man. Andrew Troller had been too calm in giving up his weapons. Too matter-of-fact, knowing there wasn't a chance to free his son now, for once the sheriff returned and someone went for the circuit judge, Longstreet was as good as tried and sentenced. Jubal moved through the intersection to Cross Street, his eyes on the family. He saw that Andrew Troller's faintly illuminated, bearded face was turned toward the west end. He and his grandsons watched a rider who entered from the flat.

It wasn't until the horseman was halfway along Grant, both the man and his claybank gelding mount clearly visible through the rain under the street lamps, that Jubal saw the rider was a black man.

He was a huge person with tremendous arms and shoulders which bulged his dark shirt. He wore a sixgun. As clearly, the deputy saw the stock of a weapon in his saddle boot. Jubal moved up the middle of the street to meet him.

The rider did not travel the length of the road. He swung in at the stage company work area and climbed down from the saddle. He looked across his shoulder when Jubal called to him.

Close now, the deputy asked, 'Are you going to stop in this town?'

'I'm lookin' for work. I hear this outfit's hirin' shotgun riders.'

He was a giant of a man, with high slanted facial bones, flared nose, and thick lips. His dark skin, wet by the rain, caught the lampglare above the barn's open doorway and held it in a sharp gloss.

'You have to turn over your hand gun,' Jubal told him. 'We have a no-gun law.'

The huge man made a slight gesture. 'I need mine, if I'm goin' to work.'

'It'll be given back to you when you need it.'

Lew Halstead, the stringy, long-faced hostler, came out from between the barn's double line of stalls. The rider wiped one hand across his mouth and flicked his eyes along the length of the street. 'I'll check mine inside, once I'm hired,' he said.

'Hired for what?' Halstead questioned. 'We ain't hirin'.'

'I was told you were.'

'You heard wrong. We only run four trips...'

'You don't hire niggers, that right!' His stare snapped from the hostler to Jubal, and Jubal saw the man's whole body had tightened. The man again wiped the wet from around his mouth. Jubal did not like waiting, but he would give the same choice here that he

54

had given to the Trollers.

'If you're going to stay,' he said, 'I'll take your guns.'

The dark face broke into a grin, but there was no mirth to it. 'You see what I got from him. I'll stop at the rest'rant and see if I'm served.'

'You will be. After I have that Colt.'

Jubal moved as if to take the sixgun from its holster, but the man was too fast. He whirled in a complete turn and brought his massive right fist around viciously to knock Jubal's hand away.

Jubal sidestepped the blow, feeling the strength of its power. The miss had momentarily thrown the big man off balance. Before he could recover, Jubal swung with his right. The blow landed solidly above the left ear and knocked the man sprawling.

The claybank stomped and jerked its head up into the rain. Cursing, the man rolled in the wet sand clear of the thumping hoofs. He scrambled quickly to his feet, rubbing the skin and hair over his ear. His deep-set eyes watched Jubal's hand, close to his weapon.

'You shamed me,' the man said. 'You saw I was turned down, and you shamed me.' He took off the gunbelt and threw his holstered .44 Colt at Jubal's chest, forcing the deputy to backstep to catch it. 'Take it, lawman. You do that to one of your own, you're askin' to be come after.'

★   ★   ★

Lightning flashed. Thunder boomed over the slopes behind the town. Jubal watched the huge man lead his horse toward the restaurant. He would be served in The Dutchman's, as Jubal and Ellie Mae had enjoyed meals there since they had arrived. Lloyd Baker, who worked the sawmill at the lumber yard had never been turned away in Yellowstone City. Nor had Roger Gabriel and his wife and children, when they drove in from their farm, had attitudes held against them because they were black. The people were all new in this land, making their own homes, and each got back exactly what he gave.

Jubal crossed Grant, his stare still on the big man, troubled by him. Jagged red-white flashes cut the air above the west end. The deep rumble of thunder was loud in the roadway. The Trollers had not moved from the hotel porch. Five of them were lined in the chairs. They seemed to watch the weather as much as they watched him.

Before Jubal reached the jail, the wind and rain struck in full force with a brilliant bluish flash of lightning and a clap of thunder that rattled the office windows. Rain poured down in a deluge, as if a great bucketful of water had been upset over the land. Jubal could hear the Trollers laugh when he broke into a run. One of the younger ones jumped to his feet to dance, slap his thighs, and howl to see him get drenched.

He slowed at the office and watched the big man open the restaurant door. Jubal's clothes clung to his body. His hatbrim dripped water. He laid the gunbelt and holster on the chair closest to the window. 'That man will be in for this,' he told Dave Ashwood. 'He gets it when he's mounted to ride out.'

'I'll see he does.' Ashwood's thin head nodded into the cell block. 'You want me to bring his meal now?'

'After the rain. I'll get it.'

'Then I'll go home for blankets if I'm stayin' the night.'

'Mr. Dillon should be back,' the deputy answered. 'Depends on how long the storm holds him up.'

Jubal stood in the doorway, unable to see anyone or anything through the dark and storm. Toward the east end the Trollers stayed outside to throw him off, he knew. Yet he was bothered more by the huge rider and the hate the man had shown, so open and cold. He was so quick to lash out. If the man had lived as a slave, Jubal could have understood. That life left its mark, and hate was a part of it. The man had such a fine claybank horse though, and a lot of gear. His clothes and gun and holster were new enough . . .

Jubal straightened to listen. He had seen the lightning flash like a whip. He thought he'd heard something, too, but the loud thunder boom, which followed drowned out the sound.

'You gonna git me food?' Longstreet Troller complained. 'I'm tellin' the sheriff.'

'Shut up!' Jubal caught the noise again, not the crack of lightning that threw bright vivid flame against the window. It was a gunshot. Its bang echoed sharp and clear through the storm.

'Don't come out,' Jubal told Ashwood. 'Lock the door behind me.'

His Colt in his hand, Jubal moved out into the rain. He smelled smoke, and then saw the glare of a fire above the roof of the general store.

The Trollers saw it. They stood at their chairs. None made a move to follow Jubal across Grant. Lew Halstead looked out from the doorway of the stage company barn.

Smoke struck Jubal the instant he opened

the store's front door, thick, oil-smelling smoke that poured from the rear of the long wide room. He expected Myron Stone would be busy with the water pails he kept in every corner. But the storekeeper wasn't in sight.

Jubal dashed past the counters. He could see fire penetrating the rear wall, tiny reddish fingers of flame which licked at the wood. He reached the staircase to the upper floor.

Through the smoke, Myron's heavy-set body was visible at the top of the stairs. The storekeeper stood with his back to Jubal in the doorway of the spare room. Myron swung about, and Jubal saw that the storekeeper held the McClain boy in his arms.

'Catch them, Jubal!' Myron called. 'They shot his father through the window! Catch them!'

Boots thumped behind Jubal. Lew Halstead ran in to help. Shouting was loud outside, then more men followed inside from the porch.

Jubal caught his breath and went into the smoke toward the storeroom. He could hear the bell in the church steeple begin to clang while he snapped the key in the lock and yanked open the door to run through and out into the yard.

CHAPTER SIX

Black, stinking smoke billowed into his face once he opened the outside door. Fire covered the doorframe and clapboards, most shooting straight up despite the heavy rain, the wind whipping gusts of flame and the filthy acrid smoke directly into Jubal's eyes and mouth.

Jubal charged straight through, holding his breath and peering ahead and to both sides. He stopped between the stone well and the barn.

Whoever had shot McClain had drenched the building with gallons of the lamp oil; he knew this from the strong oil smell and swift spread of the fire along the store's backside. There had been plenty of time for the bushwhacker to get away. The yard was almost one wide puddle, deep enough to cover all trace of bootprints.

Lights were on in the houses. Men converged on the yard. Most of them carried buckets. The first to reach the well started to draw water. Some shouted to one another; questions were called out and answered; the women and children were warned to stay clear of the fire and smoke. Jubal scanned the store's barn and outhouse and the roofs of sheds and outhouses and barns along the side street. Any of the buildings could have been used by the killer; any one of a hundred spots was perfect for a man to hide and wait. He looked at the dark figures that moved against the light of the flames, the rain cold against his face.

The bucket line was formed, the first of the water being thrown on the bottom boards.

'Get a ladder,' a man yelled 'Bring ladders to get up and knock down the fire!'

Jubal turned to the storeroom. He couldn't track the killer. It would be useless, hopeless to try. But he knew what he could do.

A skinny old man in a heavy black raincoat and with a long, narrow snub-nosed head under his sombrero called to the deputy above the confusion.

'I thought I heard runnin' through m' yard! Right after the shots!'

'We thought it was lightnin'!' his wife, as old and thin and bent as he, said. 'We didn't know a man was shot!'

Another woman, a young wife and mother who lived on the street next to Jubal's house, touched Jubal's arm and stared into his eyes. She pointed at the broken window high up on the store's backside, her face scared, questioning. 'Why? Why here? Why our town?' she asked shrilly. 'We've never had a shooting here.'

Without an answer, Jubal returned inside through the storeroom. The smoke had thinned with the doors and windows thrown open. The rush and crackle of the fire was no longer loud. The rumble of thunder and slash of rain against the building drowned out the talk behind him. The people inside the store were quiet.

They had crowded in off the porch to line the aisles under the shelves and between the counters, serious and excited men and women who whispered among themselves and craned their necks to see what went on. Others joined all the time. They pushed past the screen door and threatened to make more confusion than to give help.

Doctor Hobson spoke to Peter McClain and Myron Stone at the top of the staircase.

Lew Halstead stood with three other men at the bottom of the stairs. The body of the dead man had been carried down and laid on the landing. Owen McClain looked as though he slept. The small stream of blood that started above his left eye reddened the corner of his brow and the lines and creases of his cheek and jaw. Oakley Hall, who had leaned down to spread a bedsheet over the body, straightened. The mayor's round face was wet with sweat. He gestured toward Myron and

62

the doctor and the terrified boy in the open doorway of the room beyond the top of the stairs.

'Peter said they smelled smoke and his father looked out,' he told Jubal. 'He was shot as soon as he opened the shade.'

'Good Lord,' Harold Shanks said. 'Nobody's safe now. Not if this can happen.' He stared at Jubal. 'George Dillon shouldn't have left town.'

'He'll be back,' the deputy answered, turning to go outside. 'Move these people out of here. Tell them to stay in their homes in case anything starts while I'm out there.'

*   *   *

The rain beat down cold and icy, the flash and rumble of the storm south of the town. Muddy water pooled in the fresh imprints of boots and shoes along Grant. The water under the wheels of a wagon that drove past Jubal flowed quickly again into the ruts cut deep by the iron rims. Water dropped from the roofs and false fronts of the buildings. It seemed to pour from the overhang and eaves of the hotel, splattering Jubal's boots as he started up the porch steps.

The Trollers waited together, the six of them, two on each side of Grandpa Andrew.

63

The man called Farnley stood with Curtis Austin, the room clerk, who watched the fire with them. Jubal saw that Rolf and Zana Deistal had come onto their restaurant porch alongside the hotel. They still wore their aprons over their clothes. The huge man who had given him trouble was with the husband and wife. The three of them were as quiet and motionless as the Trollers.

'Owen McClain was shot and killed,' Jubal said to the line of men. He faced directly at the grandfather. 'The boy was missed.'

Andrew Troller did not twitch an eye. 'You look at us, Deputy. We ain't grievin'. But you can't come after us for it. You c'n see our clothes ain't wet, or our boots muddy.' He raised a hand and touched the room clerk's arm. 'This hotelman'll back us. Ask him?'

'That's right,' the room clerk agreed. 'I was inside when the shots came. They were here.'

'All of them, Mr. Austin?' Jubal had studied each pair of boots. He could not see even the slightest trace of mud.

'You saw us sittin' here,' said Andrew Troller. He brushed his silvery white beard. 'We ain't sorry McClain got his. We're just sorry he had someone else after him.'

'And that the kid didn't get it, too,' Farnley Troller put in. 'If he did, you'd have no witness 'gainst my paw.'

Jubal's eyes did not shift from the room clerk. 'What about Farnley?' he asked. 'He wasn't out here when I crossed over.'

'I was inside,' Farnley said. 'Our rooms are hired and paid for. They're ours to use.'

Jubal gave no attention to the statement. 'Mr. Austin?'

The room clerk's small body had stiffened. He nodded quickly, and answered as quick. 'He was inside. He come down the stairs when I run out from behind the desk.'

'You'd swear to that?'

Austin nodded, and seemed to relax. 'I'd swear. I would, Jubal.'

'I would, too,' a loud voice said from the restaurant porch. The huge rider had stepped close to the top step. His black eyes in his dark face bore into the deputy's. 'I don't know why you're after these people. I was in that window, and I heard the shots. I came out here and saw that clerk push past the screen door with that man.'

Jubal looked at Austin. 'You'd repeat that to Mr. Dillon?'

'What in hell you pullin'?' the huge man snarled. 'You keep pushin' people, and pushin'. I told you what I saw. I've already got reason to go after you. Takin' my gun. Now, you callin' me a liar?'

His face was purple in the light. The

65

Deistals were silent alongside the big man. Jubal heard the plop of a boot behind him, then the confused suck and pull and splash of other feet in the mud while the people left the general store. Thunder rumbled through the rain toward the southern rim as the storm moved out of the valley.

Jubal nodded to the hotel clerk. 'Come over to the office, Mr. Austin.'

'Now?'

'To talk to Mr. Dillon. He'll want to ask you some questions.'

Curtis Austin stiffened again. He eyed the Trollers, and the huge man on the adjacent porch. He took a slow stride onto the top stair and instantly backstepped out of the rain. 'I'd only get drenched, Deputy. And repeat what I told you. These men haven't caused no trouble. That's all I'd say, to you or to the sheriff when he comes back.'

Jubal watched him. 'All right, Mr. Austin. I'll expect you then.'

'Not now? After the rain, and George Dillon rides in?'

'You'll be questioned, and anyone else who might help us.' While the clerk turned toward the lobby door, Jubal spoke to the Trollers 'None of you goes where you can't be reached right away.'

'We'll be inside,' Andrew Troller said.

66

'You'll know where to find us.' He gave a flick of his hand. The others of his family followed him into the lobby, while Jubal Wills swung around to cross toward the general store.

★　　★　　★

'The man was killed!' a boy called up to Ramon Lerrazza. The Mexican pulled his horse to the right so the animal's hoofs would not hit or splash mud on the small figure that had run out to him from one of the houses 'They didn't shoot the kid, but his father's dead!'

'I will see,' Ramon answered. 'You should go in from the storm.'

'But they're lookin' for the sheriff!' the boy shouted as he fell behind. 'Everybody's expectin' Mr. Dillon!'

Ramon did not answer. He rode on into Grant Street, the rain icy and stinging against his face. He drew in a lungful of the sodden air. His heart pounded and his belly was tight. It was not that he felt blame, or had any blame. Yet he was the one who would have to tell about the sheriff.

He had smelled the smoke of the fire out beyond the town. He had seen the people leave the store and hurry along the streets, most of them returning to their homes. And

67

now he watched the sheriff's deputy cross the roadway ahead to go into the general store.

The trouble would fall on the deputy's shoulders, Ramon knew. He thought of the blood he had found inside the Pruitts' front room. The kitchen door at the rear of the small ranch home had been splintered and left open as though someone of very great strength had kicked open the lock. He had searched the yard and found a buckboard's wheel tracks dug into the grass and sod. There was no more he could give the deputy to follow.

The deputy was speaking with three men inside the store. The air was hot and smelled heavily of oil smoke and burned wood. Everything Ramon could see, the fresh bolts of dry goods, bright prints of percales and calicos, pants and shirts, underwear, bandannas, each item he and Myron Stone had marked and arranged on the counters and shelves, would smell of smoke. Mayor Hall and the banker, Shanks, glanced around at the sound of the door opening. The deputy stood so he could talk and at the same time face the street. Everett York, from the land office, was the fourth man. Ramon did not like the land agent. He was a small, sad-faced man who gave little attention to those who could not purchase land. Of the five Council members, he was the one Ramon could not like.

'Where's Dillon?' Harold Shanks asked. 'He come back with you?'

'I could not find him,' Ramon said. He told them of no one answering his knocks on the Pruitts' front door, and of how he had entered the home and found the blood. 'I followed the wheel tracks,' he said at the end. 'But they were washed out by the storm. I believe the wagon headed toward our town. That is all I know.'

'You sure you struck the right tracks?' York questioned. 'A lot of wagons and buckboards travel the road.'

'I am certain. Until the rain came.'

'The blood hadn't dried,' Jubal said. 'It can't be more than a day old.'

'Dillon could have found the blood,' said the Mayor. 'He could be out tracking.'

'He belongs back here,' York cut in sharply. 'It's Dillon's job. With that family across there, we need Dillon.'

The man looked at Jubal. A gust of icy wind whipped in through the doorway, and rain splattered against the windows. Two men walked past the store, their heads bent into the storm. Across the wide street a lone figure stood on the restaurant porch. From the man's straight posture, his big body dark against the lamp glare, Jubal couldn't miss who it was.

'Mayor,' Jubal said, 'Myron is going to stay in the room upstairs with the McClain boy. Now that the fire is out, I'm going to ask Paul Tenney and Lew Halstead to stay with them during the night.'

'That's your job,' Harold Shanks said. 'Yours and Dillon's. I agree with Everett. Dillon shouldn't be away. He should be handling the job he's paid for.'

'You should be, Deputy,' York agreed. 'You were voted in to take care of any trouble.'

'I'm taking care of it, Mr. York. I'm moving Longstreet Troller to the jail in Helena. His family will leave town as soon as they learn he's gone.'

'Alone?' Oakley Hall said. He shook his head. 'If we could be certain where George Dillon is.'

'We can't be certain.' Jubal's eyes traveled across the faces of the men. 'If something hadn't happened to Mr. Dillon, he would be here by now.'

York's bony head nodded quickly. 'They'll be away from town, Oakley. We don't want more shooting. This is the way.'

The mayor still showed doubt, and into his silence, Shanks said, 'We'll be able to send men out to look for Dillon. But only if those troublemakers leave town.'

Oakley Hall nodded. Jubal went along the aisle toward the porch. The mayor moved to follow him. York touched his arm and held him. 'I don't know, Mayor,' he said. 'We might have been wrong in our vote.'

Hall did not answer. The land agent added, 'The trouble started when Wills took over for Dillon. We've seen what happened.'

'The McClains were chased into our town, Everett. Nobody could have known this would happen.'

'You can't deny one shooting after another. I want more strength in our law so it won't start again.'

'We better think about it,' Shanks said. 'Our families have to be kept safe.'

The mayor bowed his head and stared past the window at Jubal Wills, blocking out the square of lamplight which beamed down through the rain while he went into the sheriff's office. Hall's thumb and forefinger rubbed at the hard flesh along his jawbone. 'Then maybe we'd better let the deputy know what's riding on this,' he said finally. 'He should know.'

'He knows,' Everett York said.

'I'm sure he does,' Harold Shanks agreed. 'Exactly what it means.' York left the mayor and started down the aisle past the counters, and the banker fell in alongside him.

CHAPTER SEVEN

Jubal Wills held the Winchester carbine while Dave Ashwood pulled a leather poncho on over his clothes.

'Have the Dutchman bring the extra food with the meals,' Jubal said. 'I want all our food brought in at the same time.'

'I could make three trips. It would save Rolf from getting wet.'

'Have him come with you. I want everyone to see we're giving the prisoner his meals and that we're stocking up on food. Both of you come back together.'

'What, we got you scared?' Longstreet Troller called from his cell. He leaned against the barred door where he had stood and listened to Jubal's words to Ashwood, watching them with shrewd eyes. Now he laughed. 'You are scared, Deputy. Plannin' on being locked up in here. Be damned if'n you ain't.'

Jubal turned away from the prisoner and watched Ashwood, his finger curled around the carbine's trigger. His eyes probed the alleys and doorways and windows for hidden men. A piano had started to play in the Drovers Saloon. Except for the rain, that was

72

the only sound. Dave Ashwood had almost reached the restaurant. Mayor Hall crossed the mud of Grant toward the office.

Jubal was aware of the warm sweat across his shoulders, and under his arms. Longstreet was wrong. It wasn't fear he felt. It was anger, and he was ashamed of himself. He'd handled authority before. He had made decisions. He'd had the experience and the judgment developed by that experience to give orders in the field to his troopers. Yet he had hung back from a decision today in the belief it was the sheriff who should be the one to decide about the prisoner. Or was it fear after all, that he'd do the wrong thing and his job would go? He'd seen York's expression in the store, and Shanks'. He knew.

He did know. He'd taken in Longstreet Troller little more than two hours ago. Already he showed the strain, sweating, holding on rather than acting. He had tested the chains that held the bunk because he had known what he should have done. He'd watched Curtis Austin's fear on the hotel porch. He had waited, expecting the old grandfather would act to free his son. A man had died and a boy was left without his father. He couldn't just stand and wait any longer, not sure about George Dillon, while the town grew jumpier and jumpier, with the Trollers

73

hanging over everyone and everything like the storm clouds that had hung on all day, threatening and powerful enough to explode and cause a blow-up any time they chose.

The storm was over except for the light drizzle. Jagged reddish-white flashes cut the sky above the southern peaks. The thunder that followed was a low grumble in the damp dark night which would give the cover Jubal needed. One thing Indian fighting had taught him: you had a chance as long as you kept thinking and functioning, despite the threats or wounds or the danger. Jubal spoke softly as soon as Oakley Hall stepped in off the walk.

'Will you bring your tools?' he asked. 'I want the chains that are holding the bunks.'

'Taking him alone is dangerous,' the mayor said. 'In the morning . . .'

'We'd be seen leaving in the morning. I'll have a good start before his family finds out. I'm using chains, and I know how chains hold a man. Don't let them see you crossing with the tools.' The heavy-set blacksmith paused as though he would add words, but Jubal said, 'I think they knew Mr. Dillon wouldn't be in their way. Riding in with their guns ready like that, they'll be out again if you give them time.'

He did not move while Hall left. Jubal's damp clothes clung to him. The street was

74

quiet. He could hear only the piano and the drip of water and the touch of the wind against the office window. To the east the trail that he would use was lost in the night's blackness, closed from vision until he had his prisoner clear of the town.

He and Elinor Mae had taken three days to come along that trail because of the danger to their unborn child. They had stopped the last night in a park among the tall firs, an area with ample water and grass for their horse, and Ellie Mae had rested from the long ride. They finished their meal and lay in their wagon and talked and watched the sunlight fade and the darkness work up through the high overhang of branches above them. They both had become more and more anxious and excited on the final descent along the narrow, crooked trail. And then they'd seen the Calligan Valley spread out before them.

The valley seemed larger than they had thought it would be. The Gallitan River was wider, the aspens, cottonwoods, and alders taller, the grass greener and stretching out in all directions from the small cluster of town buildings. Longhorns and white-faced cows, chickens, ducks, pigs, cats, and dogs had watched them from the meadows and fields and ranch yards as they had driven in. Cattlemen and farmers and their wives and children had waved to them. The high rocky cliffs to the north, the mountains which closed in the valley floor on all sides, made them feel as welcome and safe as the people had. They'd lain awake and talked and planned the first night in the house George Dillon had ready for them. And women neighbors had come over that next morning to make his wife feel at home...

Jubal hefted the Winchester's weight in his right hand. Hall had disappeared from sight into his blacksmith shop. Nothing stirred in the street except the wind ripple of the puddles. The piano sounded good coming through the wet. He felt a bit foolish waiting here in the open doorway with a carbine and looking around as though he expected he would be shot at any moment.

Then Jubal saw the shadow of a man move in the hotel front doorway. The middle window in the hotel's second floor showed a thin line of lamplight, and as quickly the shade was again dropped into place. He did not feel foolish any more.

*   *   *

Andrew Troller stepped back from his hotel-room window. He had seen what he wanted to see in the time he had edged the shade open.

76

The deputy in the doorway had sent for meals. Longstreet would be fed. The lights of the town made anyone near the jail a clear target. They didn't need the moon. The weather would help them, covering up sound and a man's movements. Lights, a storm, even the piano playing in the saloon, were things to be used, figured in. Plans were always subject to change. The hateful, uncontrollable anger a man felt had to be controlled when he decided to act, and Andrew Troller controlled himself. The night itself would help. He'd use lights, rain, other men, anything to do his rightful duty.

Somewhere in one of the other rooms a clock chimed the hour. The old grandfather listened, counting.

'Seven,' he murmured. He smiled to himself. They had the whole night.

He swung around and walked to the dresser. He took a bottle of whiskey and a glass from the bottom drawer and set it on the top. He know what he did. He was calm. He was always calm. He prided himself on that fact. Now he did... He could never forget the one minute he had let fear and excitement get to him twenty-two years ago. His own father had died, a McClain's bullet in him, the first Troller killed in the feud. He had been forced to look into the barrel of a rifle and stand and hand over his piece to a McClain, with his father dead at his feet. Now he had the last of that family cornered in this valley, in this town. He was calm. He waited to hear Joe Jack's footfall in the hall. He'd stay calm.

Once more he reviewed what he had done since he'd come to the Calligan Valley. The sheriff was out of their way. The people were afraid after McClain had been evened up with, despite the deputy's trying to hide him. The clerk downstairs didn't dare move, with his boys down there. The deputy wouldn't stop anything. They weren't backing down to the likes of Wills. The people who were friends of the Wills' wouldn't blame his kin. Joe Jack had made it plain he would go after the deputy. He'd be the one they would hunt...

He visualized the homes that neighbored on the Wills' house, the barns and smaller buildings and the spaces between the yards. He mentally saw the deputy and his woman in that house, the closeness of their neighbors, the distance a man would have to run to reach a horse staked outside town once a shot was fired. Andrew Troller's face was wooden, his eyes tight. The smile returned. He nodded.

Footsteps approached in the hallway. Troller turned the knob. Farnley stepped inside. 'Joe Jack left the rest'rant,' he said. 'You figure he could be backin' out?'

'He's been paid. He'll come in.'

Farnley said, 'I know that yard better than Joe will.' He watched his grandfather, his long face serious. 'I couldn't help missin' the kid! He didn't look out, but I put a bullet in where I figured he was.'

'Don't apologize, boy. Shows weakness, that's all.'

Farnley flushed at the sharp words. He went to the closet and opened the door. The wet clothes he had taken off were hung on a hook, the boots he had kicked from his feet still muddy. He took the Starr revolver he had left in the coat pocket, in his rush to get changed and downstairs and out onto the porch. Then he looked again at the old man.

Grandpa Andrew had returned to the window. His back was to Farnley. He said nothing. Farnley's hand brushed at his stubbled jaw. He rubbed at his mouth.

Farnley stared silently like that at his grandfather for another two minutes before he walked to the dresser. He laid down the sixgun and took hold of the whiskey bottle. He started to pull out the cork.

'That's not for you,' Grandpa Andrew said from the window. 'You'll have yours over in the saloon.'

Farnley set the bottle on the dresser. He flared into speech. 'You think I can't handle that deputy? I'll go through him to get to that kid.'

'None of us has to go through Wills. None of our kin.'

'I'm not afraid. You know it. I missed the boy but . . .'

'You didn't do wrong. I know how it could happen. Your paw made a mistake.'

'I didn't make a mistake. He must've ducked down beside his paw. I'd get him next time, and Wills, too.'

'I know you would. Be calm, Farnley.' He closed his mouth and turned with his grandson as the door opened. Joe Jack came inside. The black man's huge body filled the doorway, then hesitated when he closed the door behind him. He went to the dresser and picked up the Starr revolver and jammed it under his belt buckle. He gripped the neck of the whiskey bottle, making it suddenly seem small in his big hands.

'Go 'head,' Andrew Troller told him. 'You'll earn it.'

Joe Jack swallowed a mouthful. He looked at the drenched clothes and muddy boots in the open closet.

'I was out behind the deputy's house,' he said flatly. 'Not even a light's showin'.'

The old man's head nodded. 'He'd have his missus stay someplace else. He's no fool.'

Joe Jack laughed. 'He's fool enough to think I'm a drifter and bite for my trouble-makin'. The town knows we had trouble. They'll know I was after him.'

'Not just you,' Troller corrected. 'They won't be sure once you get away.'

'I want them to know. He should pay for shamin' his own.'

Andrew Troller shook his head. 'No, you'll get away and they'll follow you.' He stepped to the dresser, took the bottle and glass, and poured himself a drink. 'I want the people to think it could've been one of us, so's they'll think twice about stoppin' us when we break Longstreet out of jail.'

'There won't be nobody to stop you,' the huge man said. 'When they see what Wills gets, won't be one of them who'll dare step out of his house.'

★   ★   ★

Jubal crossed Grant Street beyond the west end of Yellowstone City.

He had left the jail office through the rear door, and had circled wide behind the town to stay clear of the business district lights. He could hear more noise now, mainly from the Drovers Saloon. Loud shouts came past the batwings, mixed with the tinkle of the piano and the occasional heavy outbreak of laughter. Lamps were on in the big, white-painted homes of the merchants. Jubal kept well away from the yards. He didn't want anyone seeing him or calling to him and letting the Trollers even suspect what he meant to do.

He turned in again close to the river. The windows of the smaller houses in the residential section were shut, their shutters drawn against the damp breeze. Jubal stopped at the end of Cross. The saloon noises were still there, the music and laughter loud, and then softer when a gust of wind blew. Except for three horses tied at the Drovers' rail, Grant was deserted. The thick blackness of the church steeple looked higher than it actually was. Beyond it the top floor and roof of the hotel blended with the steeple into a wall of darkness. He glanced beyond the river, to where the brush and timber broke off and the valley floor sloped away and rose and sloped again wide and silent until it became part of the mountain walls.

He would take Longstreet Troller out this way, and double back along the stream bed to throw off the family. He'd stay far enough ahead of their tracking to reach Helena.

He trotted through the yards and stopped near his back steps to listen. The saloon sounds were dulled by the wind from this direction. The Flannagan baby was crying while she was fed. Jubal used the loud wails to cover the click of his key in the lock. He opened the door; then, automatically, he slowed to hang his hat on the halltree.

Jubal smiled, his habit so strong from Ellie Mae's training. A dead quiet he had never before felt in his home filled the kitchen, a loneliness accented by the wind against the walls and windows. He lowered the shades and struck a match, barely lighting the turned-down wall-bracket lamp wick to a flicker. That was all he needed to collect what he wanted.

He had his poncho on and bread sliced and was taking pieces of cold chicken from the platter when a low scratch sounded at the door. His right hand dropped while he whirled on his boot-heels.

'Jubal,' Ellie Mae's voice whispered. 'Let me in, Jubal.'

His gunhand stopped in mid-air. He blew out the lamp, rushed to the door, and slipped in the key to open it fast.

His wife brushed past him in the darkness. He closed the door and she was in his arms, not kissing him but pressing herself tight and hard against his body. He held her for a moment, glad of her warm softness, feeling his need for her, fully understanding why he moved to get Longstreet Troller and his family away from everyone and everything in the Calligan Valley.

He found her chin. He took it in his fingers and raised her face to kiss her. He held her tight, and she snuggled against him. 'I watched for a light,' she said. 'I hoped you might come home.'

'I'm taking Troller to Helena.'

Her body stiffened. 'It's the only way,' he said. 'One man has been killed already. There'll be more killing if we try to hold him here.'

'You're going alone? The town men will help.'

'I could lose some of them. You know how the Trollers cut down McClain. Hate feuds aren't like handling a gunfight, or a holdup. That family will die one by one to keep Longstreet from a rope. This is the only way.'

His wife gripped him tighter, not offering an argument, simply holding him. The soft round bulge of her made him chuckle. He kissed the top of her head. A coyote howled from the streambed somewhere west of the town. Its rising, drawn-out wail broke at the end in a shower of yelps that made the Flannagan baby renew its crying.

'That's what you've got coming,' he said. 'What we've got coming.' They both laughed softly, and he loosened his arms. 'Go back to the Lashways. I'll give you time before I light the lamp.'

'You will be careful, Jubal.'

'I'm doing this to be careful, sweetheart. Stay with the Lashways 'til I come back. Keep away from the house.'

'I will, Jubal.'

He walked ahead of her to the door. He opened it an inch and listened, and studied the yard's blackness longer than two minutes before he opened it wide enough for her to slip outside. She went down the stone steps. Her shoes did not make a sound on the sand.

Jubal shut the door and turned the key. He fingered into his shirt pocket and drew out a match. He held it close to strike the sulphur tip with his fingernail.

The single gunshot outside came like a dynamite explosion.

Jubal whirled from the wall lamp. The match dropped from his fingers. The key wouldn't turn in the lock. He snapped it back, forward, and jerked the door open. Colt in hand, he charged out calling, 'Ellie! Ellie Mae!'

A shot banged, the barrel flash a stab of flame near the corner of Flannagan's barn. Jubal's hat was torn from his head. The bullet smashed resoundingly into the house's backside.

Crouching, moving forward, Jubal fired once and then again and again at the second barrel flash near the barn. He heard the bullet burn past his head, and the pained cry of a man.

Jubal tripped over the softness of something on the ground. All the breath and feeling were driven from him as though he'd taken a blow from a mighty fist. He dropped flat and stretched out beside what he knew was his wife's body.

'Ellie,' he said. 'Elinor Mae?'

CHAPTER EIGHT

Jubal's hands slid over his wife's hair, down her face, feeling the stillness of her skin. He found no pulsebeat, not even the slightest flutter in her throat. He touched the warmth of blood on her breast, directly over her heart. He holstered the Colt and slid one arm under Ellie Mae's shoulders, the other below her knees. He didn't care about the man who had run. He didn't hear what was being said. He tried only to sense some sign of life. She can't, can't die, she can't, his brain kept repeating, she can't die. He cradled her in his arms and held her tight to his chest.

'There's a man here!' someone called from off in the distance. 'He's dead! Hey no, he's breathin'!'

A woman cried shrilly, and a child's voice answered. From both the Flannagans' and Shepperds' houses, lights shone stark-yellow through the windows. Other lights, lanterns held by men and women, illuminated the yards. Jubal could see the faces that crowded around. Joyce Lashway stepped in alongside him.

'Let me through,' he said softly. 'I want to carry her inside.'

'It's Mrs. Wills,' a man's voice said, shocked. 'She's—' The words fell off in a hushed warning. 'Quiet! It's his wife. Here, open a path. Let Jubal through.'

★   ★   ★

'He's the one! He done it!' The man who shouted held a flaming lantern high above his head. Another man knelt under the light to turn over the big body of the man sprawled in the mud. He looked up, anger and hate twisting his face, his eyes finding Oakley Hall in the crowd. 'He did it, Mayor! Jubal got him! He's the nigger who threatened Jubal!'

'Get a rope!' a man screamed. 'He's still

87

breathin'. We'll string him up!' The speaker leaned over the prostrate man and reached down to grab him.

'Don't touch him.' The mayor pushed the reaching hands away. 'Don't.'

'He killed Ellie Mae Wills! He bushwhacked her and killed her!'

'He did! He deserves to be lynched!'

'No, don't go near him!' Hall's heavy body blocked the closest man, and he had to force another back. He had dashed from his home at the outbreak of gunfire, and now he watched Jubal Wills go inside past his kitchen doorway. The people stopped behind him at the stone steps. They spoke and murmured only a few moments before they turned as a single group and started to press in on the wounded killer, their talk mean and growing louder and meaner. Doctor Hobson, in a coat he had thrown on over his nightshirt, tried to move in close to the fallen man.

'Forget him, Doc,' one of the crowd yelled. 'Let him take what he deserves, what he's gonna get!' A hate-filled growl of agreement came and the men at the front surged forward.

'No! No!' the Mayor told them. 'We have to find out why he shot her! He's no good dead!'

'He's gotta pay!'

'He'll pay! He will, but let the doctor through!' Mayor Hall touched the huge man and saw that the eyes in the black face were closed. Blood drenched the shirt below the man's ribs. He had lost a great deal of blood. The top of his trousers were soaked with it.

Doctor Hobson was beside the mayor. His hands went directly to the wound. 'Bullet hit a rib,' he said across his shoulder. 'Move back and hold the lamps lower.' The rising mob calmed, but not all the talk or outrage. A few remarks continued for lynching. Most repeated what Oakley Hall had said. 'He's gotta talk! There might be more to it! He's gotta tell! Move back, make room for Doc!'

Hall watched the faces. He glanced past the heads and shifting bodies to the lighted kitchen window. The wounded man groaned and coughed, and the onlookers quieted.

'I have to get him to my office,' the doctor said. He stared up. 'You, Fred, Rolf, you men, give a hand carrying him.'

'Let him stay here! Doc, make him talk!'

'Make him! The sonovabitch'll talk!'

'Help carry him,' the doctor repeated. He straightened and motioned with his hand, his voice sharp. 'He has to be kept alive so he can talk. You men, lift him.'

Four men moved forward and took hold of the heavy arms and legs. Doctor Hobson heard the man's pained groan. He watched the man's face, the eyes still closed while he was carried. 'Jubal will need help,' the doctor said softly to Hall. 'I looked at Ellie Mae. She didn't feel the bullet. That's all I can say to help.'

Oakley Hall walked behind the doctor. A huddled form of a woman he knew was Annie Flannagan shuddered while she wept. Other women cried. Close to the house the sound of grief was loud in its silence. Those who could not watch any longer broke off and headed for their homes.

Jubal stood in the middle of his living room, motionless while Lester Dodd, who acted as the town's undertaker, draped a blanket over the sofa. Dodd said to the deputy, 'I'll take her down to my house with my wife.'

'Leave her here,' Jubal said. 'She belongs in this house.'

Dodd eyed the mayor, and he went on to Jubal, 'My wife will take care of her. Hannah will take good care of her, the way she should.' His eyes again moved to Oakley Hall, as if he wanted the mayor to speak.

Oakley Hall touched Jubal's arm. 'Jubal,' he said.

Jubal glanced at him. Hall said, 'I'm sorry, Jubal. Terribly sorry.'

A quiet came in the room. The undertaker waited, hearing the shuffle of movement beyond the open kitchen doorway. A man out in the darkness said, 'He's bad, but Doc'll keep him alive 'til he talks. He couldn't've been alone. No reason to do that 'cause his gun was took.'

Jubal looked at Hall. 'He's alive,' he said.

'Doc will fix him. You'll be able to see him.'

Jubal let out a long, slow breath. He stared down at the blanket, folded neatly, carefully over the small bulge of his wife's body. 'I want her back, Mr. Dodd. She shouldn't go from our home.'

He saw the undertaker's nod as he turned to the mayor. 'He was waiting for me,' Jubal said. 'He told me he would be, only I didn't think.'

Oakley Hall had no answer. Jubal added, 'He told me more, Mayor. Now I am thinking.' He looked once again at the sofa, and the blanket and the undertaker, and he swung around and walked out through the house's front hall.

Fred Ashwood answered the door.

The tall livery owner cracked the waiting room door only far enough to allow him to peer outside. He held his long-barreled pistol aimed. His expression softened when he recognized who had knocked.

'Jubal, I'm sorry,' he said. Rolf Diestal and the two other men in the small room with Ashwood repeated the same words. Jubal had not seen any of them in his yard. He hadn't known they were the ones who had carried the man who had killed his wife.

'Will you wait?' he asked. 'We'll need you to move him to the jail.'

Ashwood's thin face tightened. He showed the revolver. 'I thought we'd take turns on guard in here.' He glanced around at the sound of footsteps that came through the office. When Doctor Hobson appeared, Ashwood added, 'Jubal is going to take him to the jail.'

Doctor Hobson said, 'There's really no reason. He's so weak he can't do anything.'

'I want him where I can question him,' Jubal said. 'How soon can he be moved?'

The doctor turned. He led into the office. The wounded man seemed bigger, lying on the surgical table. He was unconscious, his wide face gaunt and as pasty gray as the blanket which covered him. Jubal could smell carbolic acid and ether. The man's breathing was so shallow it was almost impossible to tell he did breathe.

'You put him to sleep, Doc? There's no chance he'll come around?'

'He's out from loss of blood. I didn't have to use anything. All I could do was put on a tight bandage to stop the seepage.'

Jubal stared down at the bed, his jaw

muscles bitten together. He did not tie the man to Ellie Mae. He couldn't accept the reason this man had killed his wife. He was very tired. Too much had happened too fast. Billy Pruitt riding in and the sheriff leaving, the shooting at the McClains and the Trollers becoming such a threat, this man threatening him—and all of a sudden he went through something much more vicious and destructive than anything he'd ever faced. He breathed in deeply, thoughtfully. 'Get him ready,' he said.

The doctor opened the room's closet door and took out a deerskin stretcher. He handed it to Jubal and walked to the bed. 'Just give me time to check him.'

When he pulled the blanket aside, the lamplight struck the man's bare chest and glinted darkly on the blood of the bandage. To Jubal the slack, whiskered face was more sunken and hollow, the wide lips as pasty and still. This was the man who had killed his wife. She was dead, and this person had killed her. He swallowed against the pressure in his throat. He did not speak as he again stepped into the office and looked out of the front window.

He could not see the entire center of the business district, only to the block that housed the general store. Few people were out, the street quiet in the light thrown by the post lamps. The wind had eased down, yet water in the puddles rippled and blew; those who waited outside stayed clear of the spray.

Against the background of a porch light, Jubal saw what he looked for: a figure in a black şuit among the others. The man stood there casually, talking to no one, but watching.

'Doc?' Jubal said across his shoulder.

'He's ready,' the doctor answered. 'Fred, Rolf, you can take him now.'

Inside the office the doctor bent over his black leather bag on his desk while the men laid the wounded prisoner on the stretcher. Jubal watched the old man put in some bottles, then bandages and scissors.

'It'll be better if you stay here,' Jubal said. 'I can send Dave down if we need you.'

'I'm going along. The wound may open while he's being carried. I'll have to sew him up if it does.'

Jubal nodded. 'Straight along Grant,' he told the men. 'Do what I tell you, just what I tell you out there.'

★   ★   ★

The people moved back to allow them to go along the street. Those Jubal had passed coming from the jail were silent. Some of the more inquisitive began to trail the stretcher, their footsteps slow and noisy in the mud.

'Stop,' Jubal said before they had moved into the second block.

The doctor turned to question the deputy. The men who held the stretcher slowed. Jubal said again, as quietly, 'Stop.' He walked to the figure in black he had seen from the window.

'What's your name?' he asked.

The young man's face, half-hidden by the curled-down brim of his hat, watched the stretcher.

'Your name?' Jubal asked again. 'What is it?'

'Troller. Clifton Troller.' He looked at the deputy now, his eyes careful. 'I had the right to come out same as anyone.' From the stretcher a low, pained moan filled the instant of silence.

'You know him?' Jubal asked. He edged aside for Clifton Troller to stare into the wounded man's face.

'Jubal, he's awake,' the doctor said. 'Get him inside where I can see.'

The deputy hesitated. He repeated. 'You know him? He was on the restaurant porch when I spoke to your family. You know him.'

'No.' Clifton Troller's head shook. 'We don't know him. I don't remember him.'

'He backed your word. With the hotel

clerk. You remember?'

The boy again shook his head. Doctor Hobson said, 'Jubal, he won't live if he's opened that wound.'

Jubal motioned for the stretcher bearers to continue toward the jail. He walked away from Troller and followed along the middle of the road.

*　　　*　　　*

He had failed, Jubal was sure. When he'd seen the blacksuited man watching from the street, he had believed he'd drawn out the Trollers. If he could get only one of the family off guard an instant, just one of them to say or do something to tie this gunman to them, then he had the Trollers, every one of them.

He was certain he had failed. His mind was too confused, too pained and filled to think of another way now, while the picture of Ellie Mae lying in the mud rushed back into his thoughts. She had seemed so small under the blanket on the sofa...

He saw Andrew Troller.

The old man stepped off the Drovers Saloon porch. His young grandsons trailed him along the walk. Clifton hurried beside the grandfather. He had run ahead of the stretcher, and had told the old man, and

96

Andrew Troller had come out.

Jubal said, 'Slow, Doc, take your time. Go right through into the cell block.'

Andrew Troller reached the jail doorway ahead of the stretcher. Four of his grandsons lined up alongside him. Jubal saw that the fifth grandson stood in the doorway of the hotel with Curtis Austin. Jubal's heartbeat pounded. He crossed the walk to follow the doctor inside.

'I want to talk to my son,' Andrew Troller said. 'Deputy, you can't keep me out.'

'You can come in,' Jubal answered. The old man stepped toward the threshold and the four moved to enter with him. 'Not them,' the deputy added. 'I said just you, Troller.'

He entered ahead of the grandfather. He stepped slowly to calm the heart-thumps. He halted and waited while the men who supported the stretcher angled their heavy burden past the iron-barred doors.

Longstreet Troller, his face pressed against the vertical bars, watched the man on the stretcher. The man's eyes were open. They met Longstreet's stare. The wounded man tried to speak, but his only sound was a chattering, whining noise which ended in a groan.

'Longstreet,' Andrew Troller said.

'Don't talk,' Jubal told the old man. He had

seen Longstreet's mouth open and how his eyes switched to his father. Jubal said to Longstreet, 'You know this man?'

'No, he don't,' Andrew Troller cut in. 'We don't.'

'You can talk when I tell you,' Jubal snapped, bringing a sudden tenseness into the jail. A moan came from the man on the stretcher while he was placed on the bunk in the second of the three cells. 'He knows you,' Jubal said to Longstreet.

'I never saw him,' Longstreet stated. He lounged against the side of the cell, interested but apart from it all.

'You sure? He spoke up for your family. He knew them.'

Longstreet did not answer.

Doctor Hobson had the bandage loosened. Every person in the room could see the blood along the wounded man's ribs and stomach. The black man's face turned toward Longstreet. His lips parted, but he was not able to talk.

'The wound didn't open,' the doctor said. 'I'm still not sure of him, Jubal. He's lost so much blood.'

The wounded man's lips parted again. 'Mr. Longst ... Longst ... reet ...'

'You know him,' Jubal snapped at Longstreet Troller. 'Look at him.'

Longstreet's body stiffened. His face was calm, and he smiled thinly. 'Don't push me.'

'Why?' Jubal said pointing at the bunk. 'He earned that working for your family.'

'I tried ... I did, Mr. Lonst...'

'That's enough,' Andrew Troller cut in loudly, his voice drowning out the wounded man's. 'He was on the restaurant porch. He stood up for us, Deputy, you know that.'

'His name is Joe Jack,' Longstreet said. 'But you don't tie him to us.'

Andrew Troller said with cold impatience, 'Longstreet, shut your mouth.'

Longstreet shut his mouth.

Jubal spoke only to Longstreet. 'Anyone he worked for is as guilty as he is, Troller. You're in for shooting at McClain. I'll prove you knew he was coming after me.'

He glanced around at the line of weapons on the gunrack. 'You try to get away, your family tries to take you, one of those Greener shotguns can go off.'

Longstreet's face paled. 'That's murder,' he said in a high whiney voice. 'Paw!'

'He won't get inside,' Jubal said. 'Not one of your family will. You admit Joe Jack took your family's pay.'

Longstreet said desperately, 'Paw, he means it!'

'You were in that cell,' Andrew Troller said

in a perfectly calm voice. 'You can't be touched, son.' Longstreet shook his head, and his father spoke louder. 'We'll hire you a lawyer. You jest stay calm and keep your mouth shut. Hear?' He turned to Jubal. 'I think that clears everythin' the way it should be.'

He left the cell block and moved past Dave Ashwood and those who had carried the stretcher. Jubal followed Troller to the office front door and gripped the old man's shoulder.

'One thing you should be sure of,' Jubal said, in a strained, low voice. 'I won't stop until what was done out there is paid for. By everyone who had a part in it.'

Andrew Troller's eyes met the deputy's in a long hard stare. 'We got our rights, travelin' after that man and his son. It's our rights.' He stood there with the deputy, neither man speaking, with no need to say one more word, both understanding the other, both knowing. Andrew Troller nodded. Without a glance at his son, he stepped out onto the walk.

Jubal did not move. He watched the four grandsons fall into step with their grandfather. The onlookers in the roadway edged clear of their path as they angled toward the Drovers Saloon. Jubal glanced up at the second floor of the general store. Finally, he turned.

'Stay in here,' he said to Fred Ashwood. 'I have to talk to you and David.'

He went to the office's rear door and opened it.

The icy dampness struck his face as he stepped outside, yet it didn't help the weak dizziness that tore at his head and heart and stomach. He felt he might throw up and didn't want the others to know. The sweat drenched his body, the palms of his hands were clammy. He moved further into the dark away from the doorway.

He'd thought he had the Trollers, with Longstreet ready to admit the man called Joe Jack had come with his family. Fear had been on Longstreet's face, an expression the old man recognized. He'd lost to Andrew Troller, who would not give up his hate for Peter McClain even because Ellie Mae was dead.

The sickness came then, racking Jubal's body, and with it tears, uncontrollable, at the thought and complete realization his wife was gone from him, and with her the child they both had wanted so much to love. He wept as he never had before in his life, in a way he could not help.

CHAPTER NINE

Andrew Troller kept to the middle of Grant Street. Those who had waited opposite the jail left the walks, and the crowd slowly grew smaller. Otherwise, almost no one was in sight. The roadway in front of the big, finer homes of Yellowstone City had the appearance of a deserted town. The main sounds of life, the piano and talk of men, came from inside the Drovers.

'Clifton,' the grandfather said. 'Go into the hotel with Ulysses.'

'I want to stay with the rest of you.'

'You go in and make sure the room clerk stays shut. He'll try somethin', that deputy will. Watch for him.'

Reluctantly, Clifton continued past the saloon. His grandfather slowed until the boy was off the street. The deputy would act, Andrew was certain, right after the shock of his wife's death settled within him. The people, he did not worry about. They knew why she'd been shot even though there wasn't proof. They would stay out of it. Few men were likely to chance a shot in the dark that might come at any moment, from any spot.

But Andrew Troller's worry never had been

the people. It had been the deputy. He had figured Jubal Wills as a hard, stubborn man. He had dealt with hard, stubborn men before. He hadn't underestimated others as he had the black man. He hadn't considered Wills as intelligent or tough as himself . . . until he had stared into Wills' face in the doorway.

He had had a good look at the jail, the exact spotting and makes of the weapons on the gunrack, the desk and iron woodstove, the only two things that could be used for cover. The barred door to the cell block would be no problem once they broke in. And he had noticed the extra food and water, and the boarded window.

Andrew's respect for Jubal Wills had taken on a sudden change. He would have done the same himself, setting up for a long siege. He should have considered an Army man would think of that, but he hadn't about the black deputy. Wills had tried to tie Longstreet and every one of them to Joe Jack. The man wanted a fight, his eyes told that, and Andrew's mind had changed. His love for Longstreet and his grandsons was deep and sincere. He had planned on finishing here and bringing them all home to their women in Coleson. Wills stood in the way of that. Now Andrew held a picture in the back of his mind of Longstreet or one of the others strung up on a gallows with a blindfold over his eyes, the body limp and swinging back and forth without his being able to as much as touch it.

Andrew stopped on the saloon's top step. He nodded for the others to go past the batwings ahead of him.

The jail was quiet with no one in the doorway. Andrew felt a strange shiver pass through his body. Not of guilt, but of everything being set into motion like a trail herd he'd once seen break loose. Just a few running at first, then more and more joining until the stampede smashed and destroyed all in its path. He was calm. He didn't care about what happened to the deputy or the people or their town, no matter how much he had to smash or destroy.

'Line up on the window end,' Andrew told the others. 'He'll be comin' out. We wait, and whatever happens, let the people see it's Wills who'll decide.'

*　　*　　*

'You decide,' Jubal Wills told Dave Ashwood. 'I'll ask the mayor to swear you in if you want the job.'

Dave nodded, but his father said, 'I don't think he should agree yet. Give us time.'

'I want to,' Dave said. 'I'll only be deputy

as long as it takes for Mr. Dillon to get back.'

His father's face turned to the street. Worry cut deep lines along his forehead. He shook his head. 'Wait and think on it, David. We should talk.'

Jubal stepped away from them into the cell block. He could not take Longstreet Troller to Helena now, not with Ellie Mae lying in the funeral director's home, and with the men responsible not answering for it. He had had his time alone in the yard. He had had time to think. He would not sit and wait and be forced to wonder and guess with a thousand thoughts running through his brain about what the Trollers would do. Maybe the grandfather would try this. Or perhaps he'd do that. He might rush, or take his own time. There was no way to plan against whatever he might start, and in the meantime more people could die.

He wouldn't go through that. Dillon was still out, the Lord knowing why, and with the Trollers knowing too. Jubal stared down at the doctor wrapping the clean white bandage about the wounded man's middle. He had this killer, who knew Longstreet Troller well enough to speak his name. Now was not the time to let up. He would not rest, but only get jumpier and jumpier and the anger inside him would build and build until he grew thoughtless or careless and made the single mistake Andrew Troller waited for.

'I want to talk to him, Doctor,' Jubal said.

The doctor straightened. 'I'm going to stitch him up. I'll have to bring some more bandages from my office.'

'Yes, go ahead.' Jubal dropped onto one knee beside Joe Jack's ear. 'You can hear me,' he said. 'You had a gun. Where did you get it?'

'Not so loud,' the doctor warned. 'He's worse.'

'He's good enough to recognize Troller,' Jubal snapped. 'Joe Jack, who gave you the gun?'

The wounded man's eyes, both bloodshot, rolled to the ceiling and then focused on Jubal Wills. 'You . . . you shamed. . . .'

'You turned over your gunbelt to me,' Jubal said harshly. He touched the man's bare shoulder. 'Someone gave you a sixgun. Why? Which one of the Trollers?'

'What you tryin'?' Longstreet Troller said. 'Doc, he's dyin'.'

'You keep shut!' Jubal glared at the bony whiskered face that peered down through the iron bars at him. When Longstreet opened his mouth to answer, Jubal's right hand swept the soiled bandages together and threw them at Troller. Longstreet backed away. He brushed at the spots of blood that splattered his shirtfront. 'He's crazy, Doc! Stop him! He's crazy enough to kill Joe Jack!'

'Jubal,' the doctor began. 'I understand why you . . .'

'You don't. No one can. He was given a gun to kill me. He killed my wife. She's dead.' His fingers tightened on the dark skin, gripping until the bloodshot eyes opened wide. 'Who, Joe? I want his name!'

'Go . . . You go . . . go . . .'

Savagely, Jubal shook the shoulder. 'I know who, but I want you to tell me! I have to have witnesses and I want you!'

Joe Jack groaned, his eyes closing.

'You'll kill him,' Doctor Hobson said. He bent over the deputy. 'Not this way, Jubal. It isn't right. He'll die, and then he won't be able to tell you a thing.'

Jubal stared into the doctor's eyes, reading the shock there. He loosened his fingers and drew his hand away. Where the fingernails had dug in, the skin was swollen and purple. Jubal stood. 'I'm going to talk to him, Doctor. He'll answer me.' He walked from the cell past the iron barred doors. His hand shook. He swallowed to hold down something with a bad taste that rushed from his stomach through his throat.

'The Mayor will swear you in,' he again told

107

Dave Ashwood. 'You change your mind, that's up to you.'

Jubal saw the expression on the younger Ashwood's face, and the worried stare of Fred Ashwood. They didn't understand. They could decide for themselves. He had no intention of letting Andrew Troller have time. The old man had patience and self-control. He'd seen it on the plains more than once in a hostile chief or medicine man who knew when a cavalry troop had to slow and give valuable time he could use for his people. Calm patience, taking his own time to act. Not now. He wasn't going to be whittled down and stopped when he knew who supplied the sixgun.

'I'll be back,' he told Dave Ashwood. He reached into the rack and gripped the stub-barreled Greener shotgun. Without saying another word, he crossed the threshold and went into the street.

★   ★   ★

He saw Andrew Troller staring out through the window of the Drovers. He could hear none of the usual laughter inside, just the soft tinkle of the piano and the low sound of voices that seemed to be purposely held down and controlled.

Jubal knew why when he pushed past the batwings.

The saloon was one long room with a mahogany bar and tables spotted about the floor. The air was thick with tobacco smoke and heavy with the smell of beer, whiskey, and the half-human, half-horsy odor of the mixture of ten town men and local cowhands who stood near the piano at the far end of the counter. Gil Joyce, a tall, stout, take-your-time kind of man with balding black hair, wiped the middle of the bar with a cloth. Behind the bartender the lines of bottles and gilt-edged mirror reflected the lamplight, and the backs of the four Trollers at the window end. It was as if the saloon owner stood between his two groups of customers, separating them and holding them apart.

Jubal nodded to the bartender. He walked toward the Trollers. The town men and cowhands stopped their talk and gave sidelong glances and scowls and faint nods Jubal could see in the glass.

Grandpa Andrew was the closest, then Farnley, Calem, and Frank Troller. They leaned on the bar, their boot-heels hooked over the brass rail. Four shot glasses and one almost-empty whiskey bottle were on the counter in front of them.

Jubal stopped where he could watch the

batwings and porch window in the mirror. 'Open your coat,' he said to Andrew Troller.

'What?' Farnley questioned, his words loud. 'What are you tryin'?'

'Your coat, Troller,' Jubal repeated. 'That man across in the jail was given a gun. I want to see under your coats.'

'We ain't packin' firearms,' Farnley snapped. 'You c'n see that.'

'Open it wide, Troller,' Jubal ordered. The piano had stopped. He could feel the other eyes on him and could hear the men listening. He was hot and tired, and his heart beat a quick pulse of nausea within him. 'Turn slow.'

The old man pulled both sides of his coat high above his skinny waist. He turned. There wasn't a bulge of weapon on his body.

'You next,' Jubal told Frank Troller.

Frank unbuttoned his coat and showed his belt and shirt. Calem did the same without being asked. Neither man had a gun. Farnley, behind them, moved a hand toward his coat pocket.

'You, quick,' Jubal told him. 'Hands down. Don't touch your coat.'

Jubal stepped closer to Farnley. His heart lurched while he ran his hand across the tall man's coat. All he needed was to have one of them carrying a weapon to take him in. The

110

warmth went out of him when he felt nothing.

Farnley muttered an obscene curse and jerked his coat wide open. He held the two coattails up as though he raised both hands above his head. 'You're tryin' to pin that shootin' on us,' he said. 'We was drinkin' when the shots were fired. You ask them men!' He gestured toward the bartender and those at the far end of the mahogany counter. 'Ask them!'

Gil Joyce nodded. 'They were in here, Jubal,' he said. 'They left when we heard the shooting. They came back inside after.'

'That's right,' one of the cowhands added. He was a rider from the Huffaker ranch, a man in his early twenties whose square jaw jutted out below a twisted-brimmed sombrero that was as much a part of him as the thick black hair that showed under it and along his ears and neck. 'I saw them havin' a drink.'

'They didn't carry guns, Deputy,' another man agreed. He was older, Philip Rollins—a very neat man in his fifties who clerked for Harold Shanks at the bank. 'We'd have to back them on that, Deputy.'

Jubal felt sick. He knew he was right about how Joe Jack had gotten hold of a gun. The sure confidence he'd had when he'd entered had deteriorated. He knew he wouldn't arrest or shoot one of the family without a reason.

111

They knew it, too.

He could only keep doing what he had started. He swung around and walked out of the saloon.

He went straight to the hotel. He did not look back, going up the steps and across the porch. The grandfather and his grandsons would see where he headed. He wanted them to see and to follow him.

The hotel lobby was empty. The turned-down wick of the coal-oil lamp flickered out the only illumination in the room. Light showed from the hallway at the top of the stairs. Jubal went up slowly. His heart throbbed, his throat was tight. He had wanted to shoot inside the saloon, thinking of Ellie Mae dead in the mud. She'd been so full of life, of two lives only a minute before, and then she was dead, and the men he faced were responsible. He coughed, choking away the thoughts and feelings.

A footfall sounded beyond the landing. Curtis Austin appeared from the open doorway of one of the rooms. The hotel clerk glanced around at the lamplight that came from the room. Then he again faced Jubal.

'Deputy. I'll come down, Deputy.'

'Which room is the Trollers'?' Jubal said.

'That one,' Austin answered, and he glanced once more across his shoulder.

'They're in Twelve and Fourteen.'

Jubal nodded and passed the hotelman. The noise of the lobby door opening and then closing traveled up the stairwell and through the hall. Jubal's hand gripped the Greener stock tighter. He hoped they tried to use weapons in here, any one or all six of the Trollers.

Ulysses Troller sat on the bed beyond the open door with the number 12 painted in white on the upper panel. He was fully dressed except for his hat and coat. The door to the adjoining room was open. Clifton Troller, stripped to the waist, washed at the dresser of that room. His face and chest were soapy. He stopped and carefully watched the deputy. Ulysses was calmer. He shuffled the cards he held in his hand, his stare on the shotgun.

'What the hell you want, boy?'

'We were playin' draw poker,' Austin said nervously. 'Deputy?'

Jubal's eyes moved about the room to the bed, the dresser, chairs, and a soiled shirt and pair of wet trousers draped over a chair. 'Open that closet,' he told the hotel clerk.

'Well, I'll be one sonovabitch,' Ulysses snarled. 'You got no right bargin' in on us.' He leaned forward as if he meant to stand, but he remained seated. 'We paid for this room.'

'Open it,' Jubal repeated.

The hotel clerk looked fearfully at Ulysses and at Jubal. He gripped the knob and pulled the door open. 'Nothin' in there, Deputy. I been here playin'...'

'Into the other room.' Jubal walked to the connecting doorway and stood where he could watch both Ulysses and the younger Troller. Clifton wiped the soap from his chest. He continued to stare at Jubal, who could not see a gun or a sign of any kind of weapon in the room. 'Open the closet,' he told Austin.

The clerk obeyed. A coat and two hats hung on the hooks, nothing else. Jubal saw Clifton's eyes switch past him. He had caught the approach of footsteps in the hallway. Clifton's body was clean of soap, yet he continued to wipe at his shoulders and neck and face.

'Open the dresser drawers,' Jubal told Austin.

The hotelman did as he was told. Shirts, stockings, and dirty underwear in the bottom drawer, were all Jubal could see. He crouched and looked under the bed. He shoved the shotgun's twin barrels below the pillow and turned it over.

'You satisfied?' Grandpa Andrew Troller's voice asked.

The old man stepped past Ulysses on the bed. He halted, allowing room for Jubal to leave. Farnley and the other two grandsons waited beyond the bed. They watched their grandfather.

'We'll go to the Town Council about this,' the old man said, very quietly. He nodded to Austin. 'We have our witnesses. You're prodding us. We've done nothin' wrong.'

'They haven't,' Austin began. 'I was playin' cards . . .'

'Open the dresser in this room,' Jubal told the clerk. 'Show me each drawer.'

Austin looked at the grandfather. Andrew Troller said, 'Go 'head, show him.' When the clerk pulled each drawer open and Jubal saw each was empty, the old man added, 'That's about it, isn't it?'

'Should be!' Ulysses snapped. 'I don't cotton to the likes of him comin' bustin' in here.' He moved, kicking his feet as though he intended to stand. But his grandfather stayed between the bed and Jubal Wills.

'I'm goin' down with you,' Andrew Troller said. 'You ain't the law so you can push your way into a man's room.'

Jubal stepped closer to the bed to turn the pillow with the twin barrels. He tried to phrase an answer. He could not. The drive he had to fight on any terms when he entered the saloon and came into these rooms was still there, yet he knew nothing was going to

115

happen. He wasn't going to prove the family had caused every bit of the violence. They would laugh as they had when he'd been drenched in the storm. He could do nothing about it.

The pillow flopped onto the floor on the far side of the bed. Jubal crouched to look under the bed. His chest ached, his throat was dry. He saw only the bare unpainted pine floor— His heart slowed and seemed to stand still. Then it beat wildly. He studied the bulges of sheet wrapped around the thin mattress, each bulge an outline he was sure of. He straightened.

'Stand up,' he told Ulysses Troller.

'You bastard. You black...'

'On your feet.' Jubal back-stepped to where the pillow had been at the head of the bed. He leveled the twin barrels and reached down. With his free hand he pulled the blanket and sheets loose. Then he raised the mattress and threw it aside.

Dead silence filled the room. Ulysses looked at Grandpa Andrew. The four other grandsons looked at the old man. Austin moved away from the Trollers and the six guns, belts, and holsters which lay on the sheet spread over the bed slats.

'Pick them up,' Jubal told Ulysses. 'You're taking them to the jail.'

'He bein' arrested?' Grandpa Andrew began.

'I'm taking him to the jail,' Jubal said. 'He was the one who was hiding them. He knew about the no-gun law.' He motioned with the Greener's stubby barrels. 'Pick them up.'

Ulysses muttered a curse. He began collecting the gunbelts and weapons one by one, doing exactly as he had been told to do by the deputy.

CHAPTER TEN

Ulysses held the gunbelts, three in one hand, three in the other. He said to his grandfather, 'You goin' to let him lock me up?'

'You won't be locked up,' the old man answered. 'He wasn't usin' them sixguns, Deputy.'

'You know the law,' Jubal told him. He watched each of the six Trollers, how Ulysses waited, and how Farnley, Frank and Calem edged nearer the hall doorway so he could be blocked from leaving. Curtis Austin leaned over the bed to take hold of the mattress and replace it on top of the wooden slats.

Jubal touched the hotel clerk's shoulder. 'That can wait, Mr. Austin. I'll need a witness to back me in this.'

'I saw it. I'll have to tell what I saw.' He looked at the Trollers.

'You come over to the jail with me.'

'You goin' to keep him in a cell, too?' Andrew said. 'Why? So we won't harm him? We won't, Deputy. If you try to keep my grandson, Austin can show me who to see about bail in this town.'

The old man waited, his stare on Austin. The clerk moved around the bed and took the pillow from the floor. His fingers trembled while he placed the pillow on the rumpled mattress. He eyed Jubal and the Trollers carefully. Grandpa Andrew continued to wait. Austin's face became tragic. He smoothed the pillow and started around the front of the bed.

'I want him to get your Council members for me,' Andrew said. 'He'll be over to your jail, Deputy.'

Ulysses walked to the hall doorway. Farnley and Calem moved aside to allow him to leave. The hotel clerk's cheeks were bloodless. He would not meet Jubal's stare. Jubal paused for Austin to follow behind Ulysses.

'All I'm asking is he does that chore for us,' the grandfather said. 'That's our rights, Deputy.'

Austin looked at Jubal Wills then. 'I've got a wife and family. This is my living. I'll be over.' He swallowed. 'Please, Jubal.'

'All right, Mr. Austin. I'll be expecting you to come to the office.'

Austin shuddered and uttered a sob of relief. Jubal went past the grandfather and the grandsons into the hall. He glanced back as he started Ulysses down the stairs to the lobby. None of the Trollers had moved, he saw. He did not see Andrew grab hold of Austin's shoulder the instant he was out of sight. Nor did he see the hotelman wince at the tightness of the grip and then nod quickly to the old man's words before he hurried along the hall to leave by the hotel's rear entrance.

*　　*　　*

Jubal walked alongside his prisoner. He had the urge to hurry, but he allowed time for the fact the weight of the gunbelts and holstered sixguns slowed Ulysses. He awaited the moment he would lock the cell door securely on the second member of the family. There were five more to go. Skirmishes and battles had taught him that this skirmish would lead to the all-out battle. Andrew Troller would have to come into the open where the people would see and know the ruthless viciousness that had made him send Joe Jack to hide and wait and kill.

119

He heard the grating sound of iron on iron when he opened the jail door. Troller entered first. His arms strained, and he moved as though he intended to dump the weapons on the nearest chair. But he stopped short.

Oakley Hall glanced across his shoulder from the further cell. He had pulled one end of a bunk chain from the wall with a crowbar. His round face was shiny with sweat. Longstreet Troller stepped quickly to the door of his cell.

'They're goin' to chain me,' he told his nephew. 'Ulysses, you tell Grandpa.'

Ulysses' gaze moved to Doctor Hobson bent over Joe Jack, then to Fred and David Ashwood near the office desk.

'They're goin' to try to take me to Helena in chains,' Longstreet said louder. 'Tell Grandpa. What's the matter with you?'

Jubal placed the shotgun in the rack. 'Put the gunbelts on these pegs,' he ordered. 'You'll be in with your uncle.'

'What?' Longstreet questioned. 'What's he done? What's this boy done?'

'He isn't going to be locked up.' Andrew Troller stepped into the office. Three of his grandsons waited on the walk beyond the open doorway. The old man gestured at Ulysses. 'Put the gunbelts where he says.' His slow gaze slid across the weapons in the

Ashwoods' hands, and the bunk chain and Hall holding the crowbar. 'Mayor, I'm making charges against your deputy.'

Hall straightened and wiped one fat hand across the beads of perspiration on his brow. He shook his head to Andrew curtly. 'You're arresting this man, Deputy?'

'He had those guns. He broke the law.'

'He didn't break the law,' Andrew said. 'Your deputy busted into our rooms and took those gunbelts. He hasn't the right to do that. He isn't the law.'

'They had weapons,' Jubal said. 'You can see them, Mayor. Ulysses Troller was holding them for the rest of his family.'

'You're damn right he was,' Andrew snapped, 'with people after us.' He faced Hall, his eyes narrowed and his mouth set hard. 'What does the law read? That no guns are worn inside this town.' He waved one arm at his grandson. 'He wasn't wearing a gun. Them gunbelts hadn't been touched.'

The kick of hurried footsteps was loud beyond the office doorway. Harold Shanks and Everett York rushed past the Troller grandsons. Three town men attracted by the talk crossed Grant behind the Council members to stand in the street and listen.

'What is your law?' Andrew repeated looking at the newcomers. 'Can a man keep a

121

gun in his home or on his own land?'

York said, 'There are reasons a landowner needs to . . .'

'Does a man have the right to protect his own? What's his?'

'Well, yes.' York's bony face shifted from Troller to the deputy and then to Hall. 'I just came in. Austin told us trouble was brewing.'

Anger sharpened Andrew's voice. 'Dammitall, you're the Council, you men. You pass the laws.' He gestured as angrily at Jubal Wills. 'He pushed his way into our rooms in the hotel and took my kin prisoner. Ulysses wasn't packin' a gun. Ask the clerk. Ask your deputy if he was.'

'He was hiding these gunbelts,' Jubal said. 'The ones he's holding now.'

'That ain't the question,' the grandfather said, his voice rising. He faced Hall. 'Mayor, a man's allowed to keep protection in his house or on his own land. Your own Council member says that. Then you tell me why we ain't allowed to keep protection in our room at the hotel?'

Hall seemed doubtful. York said, 'It is your right as long as you don't bring a weapon into the street.' He looked at Shanks, and the banker nodded. 'That is how we voted the law.'

'Then we didn't do anythin' wrong.'

Andrew straightened and pointed at Jubal Wills. 'You saw us turn over our rifles and carbines to this deputy out in that street.' He motioned beyond the doorway, pausing, while two men, one mustached and young and the other as old and white-haired as himself, stepped through the crowd and came across the threshold. Both were Council members, Walter Morrell and Giles Duncan, and they halted alongside Shanks and York. Austin trailed them to the walk. The hotel clerk waited there with Farnley, Frank, and Calem Troller.

'What are you goin' to do?' Andrew went on. 'We didn't break any law. I'll see people hear how we were treated in this valley. You goin' to let that almighty deputy make his own law here?'

Shanks stirred uncomfortably and rubbed his jaw. York turned to Morrell and Duncan. 'I don't believe they've broken the no-gun law. They...'

'They came here to kill a man and a boy,' Jubal said. 'The man is dead. There's been another murder.'

Andrew swore. 'He's got no stand tryin' to tie us to that.' He pointed at the middle cell. 'That man did the shootin', not one of us. I'm leavin' this valley and bringin' back a lawyer for my son. Everyone between here and

123

Helena will hear about this.'

York said quickly, 'I think the guns should be returned to these men.' Shanks nodded. Morrell and Duncan nodded. Oakley Hall shook his head.

'The weapons are in this office,' the mayor said. 'No one is going after your family, Mr. Troller. George Dillon would hold the guns. Now that they're inside this office, he'd hold them.'

'We'll get everythin' back from the sher'ff,' Andrew said. 'Is Ulysses goin' to be locked up?'

Hall spoke before Jubal could answer. 'He wasn't wearing a weapon. He's free to leave.' The mayor saw how the deputy stiffened. 'The gunbelts will be returned at the right time.' He added to David Ashwood, 'Take them.'

Andrew's eyes switched to Longstreet, and then to the iron chain which hung dangling down from the bunk of the last cell. He nodded to Longstreet and turned his back on Jubal. Ulysses followed him.

Shanks stood awkwardly with Morrell and Duncan. York said to the Mayor, 'I want to call a meeting of the Council for the morning. You'll come out to my place.'

The Mayor nodded. He did not speak until the four left and those who had watched from outside began to move off. Finally, he turned to David Ashwood and his father. 'Thank you for filling in,' he told them. 'You were a big help.'

Jubal saw the Ashwoods' surprise. 'I was going to ask you to swear Dave in,' he said.

'No, I'm not giving any oaths.'

'But I'm willin',' David offered. 'I can do it.'

'You'd do better to take care of your own home,' the mayor told him. 'You belong there.'

David nodded, yet the movement carried no conviction. His father was relieved. He started with his son toward the doorway.

Jubal watched them leave. He did not speak.

Hall's words were quiet. 'Jubal, you would have lost if we'd forced it. We have to get George Dillon back to town.'

'Dave could handle this jail, Mr. Hall.'

'He'd be safe. As long as he's inside. What about his family? The Ashwoods aren't lawmen. The Trollers could find out where they live and threaten their women.'

Hall shook his head, silent for a few moments. 'No, this has to be done with lawmen, you and Dillon.' He watched the deputy's dark face and added as quietly and gently, 'I want to see everyone responsible pays for Ellie Mae too, Jubal. I'll stay in here, until you ride out to the Pruitts' and bring the sheriff back.'

CHAPTER ELEVEN

'We should go after him, Grandpa. Now's the time, when nobody'll back him.'

Ulysses' voice was high-pitched. His face was flushed, and he made no attempt to hide his frustration. He had stopped at the hotel registration desk, his words blurted out louder than he had ever spoken or been allowed to speak to his elders. His grandfather paid no attention to him; the old man's bent posture was in sharp contrast to Ulysses' straight stance as he watched the porch.

'You see him, Austin?'

From beyond the screen door the clerk answered, 'Wills is stayin' inside. Both of them are.'

'He'll be out.' Andrew was so sure of the deputy, he had held his family downstairs. If Wills forced another showdown, it should be in the open, where people could see and hear. Not that the chain hanging from the jail cell wall was forgotten. The picture of it was burned into Andrew's mind, the thought that

126

his son would be chained and taken away like a criminal or a slave. It was disgusting to him.

'I want a chance at him,' Ulysses said. 'Damn, Grandpa, I should get it!'

'Shut up, Ulysses,' said Farnley. 'We'll go after him when the time's right.'

Andrew waited. The town leaders had backed down when he'd told he would spread talk about their valley. He knew he couldn't trust them. If it was only a matter of Longstreet being held a few days, he might try to play it out. But the chains the mayor had freed from the wall stayed in his mind, as well as the thought of a rope noose. And a McClain was still alive . . .

Time enough to take care of the boy, time to make the deputy pay for even the thought of wrapping chains around his son. Andrew shook himself mentally, the calm inside him forcing all emotion and doubt from his mind, out of his way.

'Jubal's—the deputy's leavin' the jail,' Austin's voice said.

'Sit there,' Andrew told him. 'No reason why you can't set and rock on your own porch.'

'I want my chance,' Ulysses interrupted. 'I'll get him, draggin' me in like that.'

'How?' Farnley snapped. 'With Austin's horse pistol? It's the only thing we have.'

Curtis Austin said from the porch, 'Mr. Troller, he's crossin' to Stone's store.'

'Just him?'

'Hall's stayed inside. The jail door's shut.'

Andrew nodded. 'There are plenty guns,' he told Farnley. 'Bean'll have his rifle at the shack. The sheriff had two guns. More'll be at the Pruitt ranch.'

'Damn, then!' Ulysses blurted. 'We're goin' after him!'

'Not you,' Andrew told him. 'I want the guns here when we have to use them.'

'We should get him now!' Ulysses said wildly. 'We wait, we could lose!' He swung around and before he started up the stairs he again shot across his shoulder, 'We could lose to him! You're wrong, Grandpa!'

'You keep quiet,' Farnley called. He took a step toward his cousin, but his grandfather stopped him.

'Let him go,' Andrew said. 'We need the guns. Soon as the deputy's in the store, get your horse from the barn and leave.'

★　　★　　★

Jubal did not want to leave Yellowstone City. He crossed Grant slowly, aware he was watched from the hotel. Curtis Austin was either so wrapped up in the money he would receive for his rooms, or he was so scared, that he would do whatever the Trollers wanted. Except for the hotelman, no one was in sight toward the east end. The wind was colder. Most of the lights were out on the side streets. To the west a buggy was parked in front of the Shanks house. The Gibson boy had driven in to visit with the banker's daughter. Jubal could see the forms of a man and a woman on the long porch, the two of them clear in the shine of the front lamp.

He had been wrong, letting hurt and anger take over, so he'd gone after the Trollers. He should have stamped out the idea he could force a showdown with the shrewd grandfather. He'd felt his stand slip and then slide away from him, and he had to let Oakley Hall talk for him. The mayor's sending him after George Dillon could mean Hall had lost confidence in him . . .

He'd been hurt so much, he half-hoped trouble would come and he could prove he wasn't wrong. He walked up the general-store steps, and the street was very peaceful, very still.

Lew Halstead unlocked the front door. Two lamps burned inside, one beyond the doorway and one above the staircase.

'Tenney and I are going to stay the night,' Halstead told Jubal.

'You both have enough bullets if anyone tries getting in?'

'Myron opened his guncase.' He edged aside to allow the deputy to pass. Jubal stopped on the threshold. Halstead added, 'Ramon is upstairs, too.'

Jubal nodded.

'Nobody'll get in,' the livery owner said. 'Someone else'll have to take over in the morning. After the stores open.'

Curtis Austin had gone into the lobby, Jubal saw now. The door the clerk shut behind him stayed shut. None of the hotel windows showed a sign of a shadow. The street was empty, the lamp dark on the Shanks porch, and the Gibson boy gone with his buggy. The mouths of the side streets and alleyways along either side of the road were black and silent.

Jubal nodded and walked between the counters.

Paul Tenney slept on a makeshift bunk near the coffee counter. A sixgun and an open box of .44 cartridges lay on the counter top, and a carbine was ready within an arm's reach, leaning barrel-up against the wall.

The heady smell of charred wood became stronger at the top of the stairs. Ramon Lerrazza had placed his chair in the middle of the hall, and he waited with a '73 Winchester flat across his lap. Beyond the open doorway, Myron Stone and the McClain boy sat in the room, talking.

'Oh, Jubal,' the storekeeper said. He stood, and nodded down at Peter. 'We've been trying to decide what he should do.'

'He should stay in here.' Jubal looked at the boy. 'Don't step out of this room until the Trollers leave. Or look out the window.'

The boy's thin head nodded. He bit his lower lip.

'I mean after,' Myron explained. 'Peter has no relatives in Missouri.'

'He should stay inside,' Jubal repeated. 'I'm riding to find Mr. Dillon. I don't want you to unlock for anyone.'

He heard Myron's, 'We won't,' and said to Lerrazza, 'Ramon, would you saddle your bay and have him ready at your place. I don't want people to know I'm gone.'

'I'll be in my barn,' the handyman told him.

Jubal's eyes moved about the room to the shade pulled down as far as possible, its drawstring hooked on a nail to be certain it covered the entire window. He nodded. 'You'll be safe as long as you stay like this.' He turned.

'Mr. Deputy,' Peter said.

The boy had stood. His lower lip quivered, and he stared into Jubal's face.

'I'm sorry about Mrs. Wills,' he said.

Jubal looked at the boy, the sharp hurting ache strong in him again. Peter did not move. Jubal nodded slowly. 'You will be all right,' he said once more. 'Just stay in here where it's safe.'

* * *

He hadn't thought about the boy, after the shock of his own loss. Now Jubal could not help having Peter on his mind. Lerrazza's horse was hard to handle while he crossed the Calligan. The bay was big and rawboned, and it felt its way stiff-legged over the sandbars and had no spring once it climbed the sandy south bank. Jubal kept to the brush, avoiding the open stretches even in the dark. He had no illusions about himself. He could have been seen when he left town. The Trollers would grab any chance at him. The way the Council members had acted, his being killed would settle a lot of problems. He listened and could hear only the wind, colder and damper in these last two hours before midnight, the gusts like low long breathing that rose and fell, straining the branches of the trees and kicking up little ripples on the swell of the water.

After a mile the strangeness was gone out of

the bay. It made better time, with the jar no longer in its legs. Jubal's thoughts were clearer. Peter had no family, yet that wasn't the first problem: the boy had to be kept alive. Myron Stone would stay close to him. Everett York had looked only at Hall when he'd spoken for the Council to meet. York couldn't be depended on, nor could Shanks, Jubal knew. Giles Duncan had reacted like the banker and land agent at Troller's threat to spread talk about the valley. Duncan was old, and stooped from years of work over his jewelry-store bench. New people settling here were needed for his business. Walter Morrell depended on the same for his saddlery.

Jubal slowed the bay a quarter-mile from the Pruitt ranch. The brush thickened into clumps of sage and greasewood that was belly-deep to the horse. Rocks, from egg-size on up to boulders, blocked the trail. He turned toward the river and stopped on the banking edge. He rubbed at his face and eyes, and then at the dryness in his throat. He could depend only on Oakley Hall. The others who voted the laws were men who acted for themselves. His loss wasn't theirs. York had two sons. Neither of them had offered like the Ashwoods to help the boy. That was left to him and other men and their sons.

Someone was inside the Pruitts' home.

Lamps burned in each room, he could see once he cleared the timber on the high north bank. The bay moved faster, its hoofs making a loud sucking sound, lifting and falling in the mud.

No horses were in the yard. The barn door was closed. Nor was the house's front door open.

Jubal dismounted. He stamped the mud from his boots on the front porch and knocked.

No answer. He knocked again, and then peered through the window into an empty front room.

The door opened when he tried the knob. The oil smell was strong, as if every lamp wick had been turned as high as possible. The blood Ramon had reported had not dried on the frayed carpet. He found no one in either of the two bedrooms, or in the kitchen.

Jubal stood at the iron stove. There hadn't been a fire here all day. The fireplace in the living room had not been lit.

Then he saw the mud on the floor in front of the stone fireplace. The long rifle that had been over the mantel was gone.

Jubal took the wall-bracket lamp from the kitchen. He saw drops of mud in the rear entry. He went outside, leaning over with the lamp held low so he could run his eyes over the stone steps. He found what he looked for.

A horse's hoofs had dug holes into the mud of the yard. Water pooled in the tracks, but they were freshly made.

Inside the house, he made a search of each room and closet, and the small celler under the kitchen. He found no one. He took the lamp with him.

He moved the bay mare along slowly, his body leaning down from the saddle to see in the lamplight, his face grim. The tracks he followed doubled back over the tracks the lone horseman had made coming from the river.

On the north bank he stopped. The rider had gone into the stream to cover his trail. Jubal blew out the lamp and crouched in the saddle in case he was watched and waited for on the opposite bank. He heard only the far-off voicing of a coyote, and the uneven liquid flow of the river.

He gave the bay its head, letting the horse pick his own way through the swift, gurgling channel. He did not rush, calm in the knowledge of how everything tied together. Dillon's being called from town, the Trollers riding in with the belief they had only to find and go after their targets. Ramon had followed a buckboard's wheel marks toward Yellowstone City. The Pruitts and Dillon must be safe. They had to be somewhere close to the town . . .

★   ★   ★

Those thoughts kept coming back to him: Billy Pruitt had ridden in at just the right time, so Dillon could not refuse to leave. This was something he should have checked into immediately after Ramon Lerrazza told about the blood and wagon signs. His getting wrapped up in the McClains' fight and his emotional drive after Ellie Mae was shot had overcome his soldier-wise judgment. He knew Grandpa Andrew Troller would not give him another chance at the family. Andrew was too clever for that.

In the darkness he made slow time. The bay became impatient crossing the river below Lerrazza's small house. He could smell his barn and tugged at his bit.

'Hold it now,' Jubal told him softly. 'You'll be in your stall soon.'

The horse kept tugging. Jubal sensed something. He waited until the bay had firm footing on the bank, and he reined in.

A faint click of metal reached him from ahead, toward the barns and outhouses and homes. Fear gripped him. He crouched in the saddle and dug his spurs into the animal.

It came before he was fully ready for it, the

136

hard sharp slamming of a weapon from ahead. Jubal felt the shock of the bullet's impact along his right cheek. The next shot blasted and another smash hit him viciously above the right ear. The power of the blow drove him into even more of a crouch, the slicing pain forcing a hoarse shout from his lips. He fought for his consciousness, held on for his life.

A voice in the darkness shouted then, the words loud. Two weapons crashed together. The bullets zipped by overhead with a hateful noise of cloth being ripped. Jubal heard glass crash, and a yell off toward the houses.

He was dizzy, lightheaded. The warm stickiness of blood streamed over his ear and cheek. He could not draw his gun or grab at his head. He had no thought but to get away, no fight against the invisible enemy, no hope except to escape.

A gun flashed, and a second weapon, closer to him, as though his attackers had started their chase. A bullet struck the bay's side, thudding in like a whipcrack. The horse slowed, jerked its head high, and whinnying in panic, began to stumble. With no time to swing clear, Jubal was hurled forward, slammed down and sent sliding along the muddy ground.

He came to a rolling stop against some brush. His head throbbed, the pain pulsing with his heartbeat until it slashed through his ear and jaw into his neck and chest. Feebly, he pressed at the pain and the flow of blood. He lay there, his fingers holding tight, panting for breath, fighting to stay conscious and keep all sound down. Not knowing who or how many were after him, his best defense was concealment.

On the river bank the bay had succeeded in standing. It fled, crying in terror and pain while it trampled through the willows and down the bank to splash crazily into the river.

Running footsteps sounded. A man came through the timber to the edge of the bank. In the dark Jubal heard him call, and recognized Farnley Troller's voice.

'He's gone across . . . he was hit, the horse was hit!'

Another muffled voice answered, unrecognizable. The second man pushed through the brush behind Farnley. Jubal didn't dare shoot. He sprawled flat, closer to the earth, knowing a third and fourth and sixth could be out here. The throbbing in his head made his whole body tremble. He prayed not to be heard, holding his breath.

The men moved down the bank. Water splashed, and soon conversation and curses came from the opposite bank. Shouts and thumps of running feet sounded toward the houses.

Jubal worked himself onto his hands and knees. His hat was gone, mud clung to his hair and face, his pressing right hand was filthy and slippery. He crawled to the overhang of the banking. He had no chance in the open. One flash of a lamp and he'd be in clear view. Any Trollers hidden in the brush could finish him.

He let himself roll over the lip of the bank. As quietly he slid down into the rocks at the water's edge. The stream was cold. The wet seeped along his pantsleg into his boots. Above him the townspeople were already louder in their shouts and calls, close to the bank.

For long minutes Jubal lay still, while the hot throbs subsided. He watched the glare of the lamps and the shadowy figures which came as far as the overhang to stand and talk. Farnley and the rest of his family who'd bushwhacked him would keep looking. Then they would drift into the town and wait for him. But he would never reach the jail.

He lay there hugging the dark rocks for longer than a half-hour. Mud covered the bullet wounds, but the warm sticky seepage hadn't stopped. Gradually the confusion in the timber and brush quieted. The townspeople could learn no more about what had happened. The last of those who'd brought out lamps returned to their homes.

Jubal crawled slowly up the bank. He sprawled flat to regain his breath. He had to get where he could rest. Most of the lights in the houses were out. He studied the dark irregular outlines of the roofs, and he thought of Lerrazza. Myron Stone's handyman was the best chance. He decided to make his run.

He crawled to the edge of the brush. Alongside a large cottonwood, he lay without a move and regained his breath. Finally he stood, pressing the hairline above the ear. He bent low and began to run. He crouched again, panting heavily while he rested near a pile of rubbish and lumber behind the closest barn. He continued in this fashion and, groping his way, made progress between rests. When he reached Lerrazza's barn, pain knifed through his head and neck and his breath wheezed in ragged gasps.

He stumbled to the house's rear door and knocked. A lamp was lit inside. He knocked again. Bare feet padded on the floor. 'Who is it?' Ramon's voice questioned.

'It's Jubal, Ramon.'

'Who? Who is there?'

'Jubal, Ramon. I've been shot. It's Jubal Wills.'

The iron bolt clicked. In another moment

the door swung back and Lerrazza peered out.

'What is...?' Ramon swallowed and stared wide-eyed at Jubal. 'Oh, dear Mother in Heaven!' he breathed.

Ramon took hold of Jubal's arm and helped him past a kitchen table and warm stove into the bedroom. He smoothed the blanket and pillow and helped Jubal lie down. Gently, he lowered Jubal's hand from his head. Two wounds, he saw immediately. The bullet that had struck above the ear had ripped a bone-deep six-inch gash in the hairline. Mud and caked blood filled the wound. The cheek was not as deep and half as long, but just as filthy with mud.

'I will go for the doctor,' Ramon said.

'No—not the doctor.'

'You have very bad wounds. Covered by mud. Without the doctor, they will become infected.'

Jubal began to shake his head, and the movement shot pain through his ear and neck. He lay absolutely still. 'You clean them, Ramon. Do the best you can.'

'But Jubal...'

'They bushwhacked me. They'll watch the doctor. If you brought him, they'd kill all of us.'

Ramon shook his head.

'I saw one of them. Farnley Troller. Others

141

were there. They couldn't find me, so they'll keep watchin'.' He exhaled deeply and let his eyes close, exhaustion taking hold of him. He heard the shuffle of bare feet again and opened his eyes and turned his head.

Ramon stood at the stove. The small Mexican poured water from an olla into the kettle. He opened one side of the stove and added wood.

Jubal lay quietly and let the throbs that had started subside to a steady painful pulsebeat. His gaze traveled about the bedroom to a bureau and nightstand and a cane-backed chair. On a shelf a wooden image of the Virgin of Guadalupe stood between two candles. His eyes studied the statue when Lerrazza returned to the bed. The Mexican held the kettle, a bowl, and a bedsheet.

'This will hurt,' he said. 'I do not have whiskey.'

'I don't want any. In case someone comes.'

'I could tell Mayor Hall.'

'No. He can't open the jail door.' He explained what he had found at the Pruitt ranch, and how he had been shot. 'I have to be the one who takes Troller in. There's a hundred places Dillon and the Pruitts could be. I've got to find out where.'

Ramon nodded, his face sober. He stepped away and opened a drawer. He placed a small

142

knife and a spoon in the basin and poured the steaming hot water over them.

'Turn your head to the side,' he said. 'Toward the wall.'

Jubal obeyed. Ramon used the spoon and large bandages ripped from the sheet to wipe the mud from his cheek. Jubal's body shivered when the Mexican began to clean above the ear.

'This is deep, Jubal. The doctor should . . .'

'You do your best. You, Ramon.'

Ramon tore the sheet into smaller pieces and then went to work on the wound. The touch of the hot cloth brought pain, the rubbing an agony. Jubal clenched his teeth together and held his body stiff, but nothing could control the shuddering.

For longer than a half-hour the Mexican cleansed the wound. He worked very slowly, taking care with tender hands and plenty of hot water, easing up when Jubal's body shivered, or the muscles in his wide jaw and neck hardened and strained against Ramon's hand.

Finally, he stopped and looked from the two wounds to Jubal's eyes. 'They are as clean as I can make them without causing more bleeding. You must have the doctor.'

'When the sun comes up. When anyone can

be seen waiting for us.'

'Mud is still in the hair, Jubal. It's not all out.'

When Jubal said no more, Ramon put a bandage on the cheek. He packed the tear above the ear and cut the rest of the sheet into strips to bind the wound.

'You have to sleep now,' he said. 'I'll sit with you.'

Pain still throbbed in Jubal's head, and his ear ached. His lips were dry.

'I'll make coffee,' Ramon told him.

'Not coffee. Just cold water. A little.'

Jubal pushed up so he leaned his back against the bedroom wall. The dizziness settled. The water was chill in his mouth, but it quieted his insides. After a few minutes, he said, 'I want to talk to Austin from the hotel before I see the doctor.'

'You can't go to him. Not with that family watching.'

'He would have seen the Trollers leave the hotel. I need him. I have to get him away from them.'

'I'll bring him back for you.'

Jubal nodded, drowsy.

'I'll tell Mr. Hall,' said Ramon. 'He'll ask men to help.'

'You can't go near the jail, Ramon. That old man would send some of them down to check this house.' For a moment, thinking, he was silent. 'It has to be done careful.'

'Yes, Jubal.' Ramon placed a hand on Jubal's shoulder. 'You rest.'

Jubal wanted to go on and tell exactly what he wanted, and to think about where Dillon and the Pruitts might be. He could not put his thoughts into words. Exhausted, he lay back.

CHAPTER TWELVE

The people had turned out the lights in their homes and returned to their beds, but that gave Andrew Troller little satisfaction. He had stood for the last forty minutes inside the darkened hotel barn, listening through the open rear doorway. The overcast made a black night, yet he could see the hazy silhouettes of houses and the top of the timber along the Calligan. Once again he could picture the river, with Farnley and Ulysses hidden and waiting. It was foolish, what they had tried. It could still wreck everything he had set up.

The deputy might have expected a bushwhacker. After seeing nobody was in the Pruitt house, and the guns were gone, Andrew would have watched for a bushwhacker himself. A sergeant in the Army who had spent time in Indian territory, would have been cautious from experience. The boys should have come to him. They should have asked.

Somewhere beyond the doorway boots or shoes squelched the mud. Andrew listened. Whoever it was approached from the flat, not from the town.

Clifton said behind his grandfather, 'Think it's them?'

'If it ain't, you remember, they left to ride to Helena,' Andrew answered quickly. 'We're waiting for them to get back.'

Andrew's vision separated the darker figures from the land. He recognized Farnley's tall, slightly bent way of walking. Ulysses was directly behind him. Andrew felt relief, but the impatience to know what had happened kept him cold inside.

The two meant to pass the barn and head for the hotel. Andrew saw for certain they were his grandsons. He said in a low voice, 'Farnley, get in here.'

Farnley's shadow stopped. Ulysses stopped. Some words passed between them, and both moved at a hurried walk through the doorway.

Their grandfather closed the door and lit a lamp. His two grandsons stood rigidly. A long rifle was in Farnley's hands. A holstered Colt sixgun was belted about Ulysses' waist.

'Well?' said Grandpa Andrew. 'You mean to wait all night?'

'I think we got him,' Farnley began.

'You think! Dammit, boy, ain't you sure?'

'We hit him. I'm damn sure from how he yelled.' He continued to talk, watching the old man's angry expression. 'He was thrown when the horse went down. Could've been into the river and he drowned.'

'I think he was,' Ulysses put in. 'We got him. We killed his horse. We tracked it into the meadow and found it dead. It hadn't run a half-mile. Our bullets went into him.'

'One of your bullets went into a house,' Andrew told them sharply. 'Good thing for you nobody was at the kitchen sink or the whole town'd been after you.'

'We didn't know,' Farnley said. 'Wills tracked me, Grandpa. I'd jest got out of the Pruitts' when he rode in. He went into the river where I did. I didn't have time to wake you. All I could do was take Ulysses with me and go and wait for him.'

Silently, Andrew studied them. His cold impatience had quieted to calm thought. The deputy could be dead, or he could have dropped off the horse anywhere between the river and the meadow. If there was no way for Wills to prove who had done the shooting, he

147

could make certain his family wasn't blamed.

'Them guns'll go in the hole Clifton dug in the back stall. Give them to him.'

'We need guns—' Ulysses began.

The grandfather slapped out with his hand and caught Ulysses full across the mouth. He saw the boy's shock, and a reddish welt begin to swell at the corner of his lips. 'You'll bury them,' he ordered. 'If Wills is alive, he'll check our rooms and these horses. Clifton's wrappin' canvas around them for when we need them.'

He turned down the wick and went outside and walked to the hotel's rear door.

Curtis Austin was behind the registration desk. Frank Troller was with him, staying close, as he had been told. Andrew walked past them without a spoken word.

He climbed the stairs to his room. A man came out of one of the other rooms while Andrew turned the key in the lock. Andrew nodded to the man and said, 'Looks like its goin' to clear before mornin', and he nodded again to the man's agreement. Andrew's stance was calm, relaxed, his voice casual. Once he closed the door behind him, his features took on an abrupt change.

He swore to himself and put a match to the wall lamp. He drew in a ragged breath and began to walk about in tight circles. He had

had Wills on the run, but the shooting could have changed that. He would know when the day started in the town. He had to wait and see how the people were, how they talked. He stopped his walking and went to the bottle and glasses on the dresser. He poured a glassful of whiskey. The liquor spilled and he wiped it with his kerchief. He was careful not to leave one drop of liquor to stain the painted top.

He stepped to the window and opened the bottom half to let in air. Then he stared down at the street. For several seconds he remained motionless, his body slumped forward. Nobody was in Grant. The jail door was shut. He was to blame, not the boys. He should have stayed awake and not had Ulysses wait for Farnley. He wouldn't have allowed them to leave if he had been the one who watched Austin. He never would have hit Ulysses. He never had before, never had been forced to.

Somewhere in one of those close yards a dog barked and a cat screeched. The remote, wild noises only emphasized the silence of the room. There was a fight which went on out there between the animals, and a war was ready to start further west on the plains, with General Custer building his troops at Fort Abe Lincoln and the Sioux getting as ready under Crazy Horse and Sitting Bull. Everyone knew it and allowed it, yet because of one black lawman he couldn't carry on his own fight.

Andrew rubbed his thumb and forefinger of his right hand along his jawbone. Suddenly, when he became aware of what he did, he flung the hand away from his face. It was a nervous habit. He could not afford to be nervous.

The door opened behind him. Clifton's voice told him, 'They're buried.'

'We can get them when we want?'

'All we do is dig up the canvas.'

Andrew Troller nodded. 'Tell them to sleep. They get their rest while we wait.'

Sleep came fitfully for Jubal with his dozing and waking at intervals. The pain lessened gradually, and left only a throbbing that quickened if he moved. All during the night he was aware vaguely of Lerrazza's presence, that the Mexican's face was often close when he was given water or something else was done to make him more comfortable.

When Jubal woke, the night had started to brighten beyond the window. It was the dull light of an overcast sky, but it steadily gave way to day. He rolled onto his back and edged his body onto one elbow.

Ramon's eyes opened where he sat in the cane chair. 'You need more rest,' he said.

'I have to talk to Austin. Go for him, before the Trollers are up.' He pushed himself onto both elbows. He still was weak. His head and ear thumped with a slow, steady rhythm. 'Go through the store, as though you want Austin to come over there and talk to Myron Stone.'

'I will bring the doctor.'

'Just bring Austin,' Jubal said. He rubbed his forehead to ease the ache.

Without answering, Ramon poured coffee into a mug and handed it to him. 'This will help. I will knock three times,' He eyed Jubal's holstered sixgun draped over the bedpost as he turned the doorknob. 'Three times, Jubal. I will unlock the door.'

'Thanks, Ramon. If you're followed, head for the jail and tell Hall.'

Jubal moved his legs off the bed and sipped the hot coffee while the throbbing his motion brought subsided. He stood, dizzily, and after a few minutes that also calmed. He buckled on the sixgun. Its weight had never been so heavy, or the bulk of the belt and holstered weapon so awkward.

He finished the coffee and had his boots on and was cleaning the dried mud from his shirt and trousers when he heard sounds outside the house.

Jubal loosened the sixgun in the holster. He poured more coffee, then sat, his spine pressed against the chair's cane back.

Three knocks came. A key was inserted and

clicked in the lock.

Curtis Austin followed Ramon inside. The hotel clerk's eyes widened when he saw Jubal. He swung around to wait for the Mexican. 'You said we were gettin' somethin' to help the boy.'

'We were not suspected,' Ramon told the deputy. 'The young Troller slept in the lobby. He did not try to stop us.'

'Which of the Trollers left town last night?' Jubal asked the clerk.

Austin's bald, bird-like head shook. 'None at all that I know of.' He fingered his gold watch chain. 'I don't see everyone who comes and goes.'

'One of them did leave then?'

'I don't know. I didn't see any.' He stared from Jubal to Ramon Lerrazza. 'Some of them did go outside when the shootin' started. Grandpa and Clifton. They stayed in the yard. I think...'

'You think. You think!' Jubal said cutting across his words impatiently. 'Shooting broke out and they looked to see what it was like everyone else?'

'As far as I know. Listen, don't tie me in on this.'

The deputy eyed him silently. 'Ramon, my hat's in the brush. See if you can find it, and bring the doctor to the jail.' He finished the last of the coffee while the Mexican left. The hot liquid did not help the soreness.

'You're covering for that family,' he told the hotel clerk pointedly. 'You think that will keep you safe? You really believe your family will be safe once the Trollers are shoved into a corner?'

'I'm not part of your trouble.'

'You are, Mr. Austin. Every person in this town is. Every person in this valley. The Pruitts aren't in their home. Mr. Dillon isn't out there. They were taken by someone.'

Austin glanced away, avoiding Jubal's eyes. 'I don't know about that. They haven't talked about that.'

'They have talked, though? You heard them?'

Austin shook his head. 'Not in front of me. All I know is they hired my rooms. I have a right to make a living, and think of my family.' His lips tightened together and he watched Jubal defiantly.

Jubal stood, aware of the soreness more because of his anger and frustration than from the movement. He said, 'You can't keep your family safe like this. I couldn't. No one can.'

Curtis Austin was silent, as though he had not heard.

'Wait with me,' Jubal said. 'When Ramon comes, we'll go up together.'

CHAPTER THIRTEEN

The air was chill in the Shiloh Hotel Lobby. Andrew Troller barely noticed. His bony figure, dressed in his black suit and black hat, stood tall and straight while he watched through the screen door. He studied the length of Grant, the store buildings and big fine homes of the west end, the smaller houses, the timber screen along the Calligan, and the land all gray and dull under the overcast which hung on and showed no sign of breaking. He saw the thin columns of smoke which rose here and there from chimneys. People were having breakfast. It was perfect. Most would be inside out of his way, but that did nothing to change his stern expression.

'Grandpa, look 'longside the hotel,' Calem said, and Farnley muttered, 'So that's where he snuck to damn him!'

Andrew's brief glance down the general store alley weighed what they saw. Jubal Wills, his face and head bandaged, Stone's Mexican handyman, and Austin walked together toward the street.

'That sonovabitch clerk,' Ulysses snapped. 'If the bastard talked.'

'Look ahead,' Andrew ordered. 'We'll all

154

go out, and act natural. Austin knows what I said 'bout his family. He hasn't opened his mouth.'

Ulysses looked at his grandfather worriedly. 'We should've gone into the houses, dammit. That rotten Mex.'

'Close your mouth, boy. Close it. Men are coming from the houses. Don't let them see anything bothers us.'

Ulysses became silent. When his grandfather opened the screen door, he and the others followed onto the porch.

The three town men who had come out of their homes turned into Grant. All saw the Trollers appear on the hotel porch. One of the trio was Philip Rollins, the bank teller. He was the first to see Jubal Wills step from the store alley.

'What happened down there?' he asked.

'It's the deputy. Looks like he was the one who was shot.'

'Bad? He's covered with mud. I wonder how bad.'

'Can't be too bad. He's walkin' by himself.'

The three moved along the boardwalk, aware that the deputy had seen the Trollers. Jubal Wills cut across the width of the main street straight toward the hotel. The door to the land office opened. Everett York had evidently slept inside. The land agent hurried down to Rollins and the other two watchers.

'You men stay with me,' he said.

'It's not my trouble,' Rollins answered. 'I'm not getting caught between them. None of us wants to be.'

'I'll tell that to Harold Shanks,' York said loudly. He eyed Rollins' companions. 'This town loses its good name, we all lose.'

The bank teller did not answer. The others grew as instantly uneasy, and the three trailed the land agent.

The Trollers on the porch waited quietly. Curtis Austin dropped behind the deputy and Lerrazza. Jubal halted at the bottom step and stood with his gun hand inches above his holster. In the moment of silence a window went up on the hotel's second floor and from the adjacent restaurant came the faint scraping of shoes on that porch.

'Farnley Troller,' the deputy said. 'Come down here.'

'I got no reason to, mister.'

'There's reason. I'm taking you in.' He was aware the four men had crossed behind him, and that now both Rolf and Zana Deistal listened from their porch. 'You bushwhacked me last night.'

'He did not,' Andrew snapped in a loud voice. 'This is more of your pushing, Wills.'

'Farnley was the man who shot me,' Jubal

156

said as loudly. 'He was seen at the river. Someone else was with him, but Farnley can be identified.'

'Identified—' Andrew repeated. He could not hide his surprise while his stare switched to Austin.

The hotel clerk said fast, 'It wasn't me. I didn't tell anythin'. I didn't know Farnley was out.'

Andrew nodded at the statement. 'He'll say we were in the hotel. We have our witness.'

'Then a judge will decide,' Jubal told him. 'I saw Farnley in the brush. I can tell you the exact words he spoke.'

The statement brought low talk from the watchers. Andrew's glance flicked from the deputy to the onlookers, and then to Austin. The hotel clerk, not sure of himself, said, 'Ramon told me I was needed in Myron's store. I didn't know...'

Everett York interrupted. 'You can't be your own witness, Deputy. It's their word against yours.'

'I'll identify Farnley,' Jubal said, his eyes on Andrew. 'He'll come with me, Mr. Troller, or I'll take him.'

'You're picking us up one at a time,' Andrew snapped. 'Because your wife was shot, you'd go to any length to get my family.' His gaze moved to York, as though he expected the land agent or one of the businessmen would add something. York was silent, his attention on the seventh and eighth town citizens who joined the crowd.

A sudden troubled expression lined Andrew's face. It vanished as quickly as it had come. But the change was enough for Jubal. He held his voice calm. 'Farnley, step down. I'll use my gun if I'm forced to.'

'I c'n prove you're lyin',' Farnley said. 'Austin'll say I was in my room.'

'He can appear at the trial.' The deputy's voice hardened. 'I'll identify you, and you'll answer to our law.'

Other voices echoed his words. More townspeople were joining the watchers, serious-faced people whose eyes widened when they crowded in nearer and saw the deputy's bloody bandages and mud-caked clothes.

'Try to take me,' Farnley said. 'We ain't got guns but we'll fight.' He looked at his grandfather.

Andrew wasn't looking at his grandson. His mouth was tight, and his eyes were cautious while he surveyed the spectators. 'Go with him,' he said.

'What, Grandpa—'

'Go with him. You done no wrong, but we obey the law. We have, we do now.' His

158

fingers rubbed vigorously along his jawbone. His voice pitched low, he snapped, 'I've talked enough.' His gaze bore into Everett York, then raked the watching faces. 'I'm not goin' to do any more talkin' in this town. I'll talk, but not in this town.' He swung about and grabbed hold of the door handle.

The crowd was frozen, watching the old man and his grandsons leave, and Farnley stepping down to the deputy. York hurried across the stairs and porch and caught the screen door before it swung shut. He ran through the lobby after the old man.

'He'll be given a fair trial,' the land agent said. 'We'll see it's fair. Our Council will.'

'You won't do one damn thing.' Andrew did not slow until he reached the registration desk. Austin had followed York. The clerk scurried around behind the counter and picked the room keys from the rack.

'I'll appear for you, Mr. Troller,' Austin said. 'I didn't tell anythin'.'

'You'll get fair trials in our town,' York was saying.

'We'll get nothing but jail in your town,' the old man spat. 'But I tell you it doesn't stop now. I tell you!'

He turned his back and climbed the stairs, aware that his grandsons stayed behind him. He jammed the key into the lock, snapped it,

159

and slammed the door in against the wall.

'Get your horses,' he told his grandsons.

Ulysses said, 'We dig up the guns?'

'Clifton does.' He looked at the youngest, beardless smooth-skinned face. 'You know where Austin's family lives. You know what I told you. Go 'head, all of you.'

Andrew whirled on his bootheels and pulled open the middle dresser drawer. He gripped the cap-and-ball pistol they had taken from the hotel clerk, and he laid the weapon on the bed. He stared at his hand. His fingers shook. He cursed obscenely, and gripped his hands together to stop the shaking.

He went to the window and stared out. The doctor, carrying his black bag, went toward the jail, past the people in the street. Two men on the general store porch looked up at the window. Andrew did not pull back. The sheriff's office door was open, from the way people near there stayed close to the jail. The deputy wanted everyone to know he had his second Troller prisoner. Wills played that out exactly as he had played out the talk in the street, bloody and bandaged and filthy with mud and using that to get the people to back him.

Andrew swore silently and massaged his jawbone with his fingers. The satisfaction he'd had evening things with Owen McClain was gone. The fear he'd put into the last of the hated family, the fact he knew he would kill the boy and finish the feud, his making up for having to hand over his weapon with his own father dead so many years ago ... all were forgotten. He had to bring Longstreet and Farnley home. Their women would never forgive him. He could do it, and settle for once and for all with Jubal Wills and the rest. There was a way he could.

Andrew realized he was again rubbing his jaw. He doubled his fist, tightening until pain shot sharply along the tendons of his wrist.

He shivered, enjoying the pain, and tightened his fist more. His body bent forward and he moaned deep within his throat. His forehead pressed the window, and the cold of the glass burned against his skin. The moan came out louder, growling like some vicious animal.

CHAPTER FOURTEEN

'Stay still, Jubal.'

Doctor Hobson's head leaned over Jubal, the iron-rimmed glasses on the end of his long nose close to the cheek wound. Jubal held his breath to not inhale the strong carbolic acid

fumes. He flinched at the sharp jabs of pain
the doctor's rubbing brought, trying to keep
his eyes on Oakley Hall while he told the
mayor what had happened with the Trollers.

With Farnley locked in the last cell, the
next play was up to the grandfather. Jubal
winced at a flash of pain. He kept his face
grim, thankful that Andrew Troller, despite
all his cleverness, knew so little about the
military tactic of using an enemy's own
weapons. The people had been the old man's
strength. He had turned that strength into his
own at the hotel porch. He had seen that even
more clearly himself while he told Hall.

'The tracks didn't come out of the river?'
the mayor said now. 'You can't prove they led
back here?'

'The shooting proved it,' Jubal told him. 'I
was too close to what I wanted.'

'Not with me, you weren't,' Farnley
snapped from his cell. 'You can't prove I was
at the river.'

'He was there.' Jubal stared at Hall and
straightened in the chair as the doctor pressed
a bandage against the cheek.

'Hold this,' Doctor Hobson said. 'It'll keep
the dirt out while I look at your head.'

'Wait, Doc.'

Jubal stood quickly, the pain forgotten.
Beyond the open office door the street was
162

brighter from the first sign of the sun breaking through the clouds. The four horses and riders turning in toward the tierails threw a hazy shadow. Andrew did not wait for the younger Trollers to rein in before he dismounted and stepped across the walk.

'I want to talk to my kin,' he said.

He did not look at the doctor or the deputy. His stare swept past Hall and Ramon Lerrazza. He gave no attention to Joe Jack, only to Longstreet and Farnley behind the iron bars. He walked to the center of the corridor and faced his son and grandson. 'You'll be out. Both of you, hear?'

Longstreet grinned, and Farnley answered, 'We hear, Grandpa.'

'You're all right, Son.'

'Fine, Paw.' The eyes above the grin moved to the deputy. 'He was shot by somebody. Reckon he's got the same bad enemies as McClain.'

Andrew did not answer. He turned, and now his stare met Jubal's. 'Law says our guns are given to us when we leave. We're leavin'.'

Jubal hesitated. The Trollers and the horses had been joined by a spotting of the curious. He hadn't expected this. The Troller family did not back off like this.

Hall took five gunbelts down from the wall pegs. The mayor nodded toward the rifle and

163

the carbines stacked in the far corner of the room. 'Ramon, help me bring these out.'

The grandfather went past Jubal. He swung up into his saddle and did not speak a word while the gunbelts and rifle and carbines were handed back to first one member of his family, then to the others.

Jubal stepped through the doorway onto the walk. He stood in the open, his gun hand inches above the handle of his Colt. His eyes watching the grandfather, aware the grandsons buckled on their weapons, Jubal adjusted the hang of his holster.

'Clifton's not with you,' the deputy said. 'His guns aren't his if he isn't leaving.'

'He's already left,' Andrew stated flatly. He handed Frank the extra carbine. Holding the extra gunbelt in one hand, he turned his horse. The others turned their mounts with him and they rode into mid-Grant toward the west end.

Jubal's fingers brushed the bone handle of his Colt. He waited for them to pivot their animals and swing about, spreading out. None of the black-suited backs as much as shifted position in the saddles.

'I'll go to the Dutchman's with Ramon and bring food,' Hall said. 'After, you'll want to rest, Jubal.'

Jubal nodded. He returned to the chair and

bent his head as he sat.

There was more pain when the doctor touched the wound above the ear. Jubal sat stiffly and listened for some sound to warn him the Trollers were coming back. But he heard nothing except his own slow, steady breathing.

He did have to rest, he knew. He knew he did not want to go to his house and be alone, not now when not one thing had been settled. Andrew had made a promise in the cell block. He would try to keep it.

Jubal nodded to himself. Doctor Hobson said, 'Don't move. I'm about done,' and Jubal sat still. He could not go home without everything finished. To him, Ellie Mae would be in each room, her likeness on the mantel smiling at him, her chair opposite his at the fireplace, the sewing patterns and cloth for the baby clothes exactly where she had left them. They had been here such a short time, and had had such a short life together. He had nothing now. Life had been one person to him. Life wasn't just getting a job, and the security they had talked about so often. Life was love, the love of one person, of one for another, and when that person died, you died too.

Doctor Hobson dropped the bloody, mud-streaked cloth into the basin. 'It's clean,' he said. 'I'll want to check the bandage tonight.'

Jubal straightened. The pain stopped while the bandage was wrapped tight, but it could not stop his thoughts. He could not help seeing the fine, long-legged girl who had cleaned the tables and dishes in the San Antonio cantina. She had seen too many soldiers, and had been hard to get to know. She had seen too many wives widowed. He had walked with her to her room when his troop was in. Their relationship was friendly, nothing more. That's all they said it to be . . . Until one night, when the moon had been bright and he had looked at her during a lull in their talk. Her quiet face had been clear in the silvery light. They stopped, and he put his hands on her shoulders and she moved so easily, so tenderly into his arms. He took this job in Yellowstone City. The pay was enough to care for a wife and the family they wanted . . .

'Eat this,' Oakley Hall said holding out a plate of eggs, steak, and potatoes he had brought into the office.

Behind the mayor, Ramon carried two more plates of food. Everett York held a plate of bread and a large pot of coffee.

York went into the cell block and passed the bread through the iron bars. 'You have mugs,' the land agent said across his shoulder. 'I'll fill them for these men.'

Jubal cut the steak. A throb nagged at his jaw while he chewed.

Ramon brought him bread and coffee.

'Will you help the doctor feed Joe Jack?' Jubal asked the Mexican. The wounded man's eyes were open on the bunk, watching them.

York said to Longstreet Troller, 'We'll see that you're well fed. If you want more, we'll bring it.' He turned to Hall. 'Have you told him, Mayor?'

Hall said, 'In my office, Everett. We'll go across.'

'I don't see why,' the Council member answered. 'When a man is wrong, he knows he has to answer for it.' He looked at Jubal. 'We're holding a meeting today. You haven't handled the law the way George Dillon did, Deputy. George didn't make violence.'

'The violence wasn't mine, Mr. York. My duty is to stop it.'

'Those two men you've locked in here haven't been proven guilty. They will be treated decently in this town. I intend to see to it that any person will be treated decently.' He paused at the quick thump of boots on the walk beyond the doorway.

Curtis Austin ran into the office. He looked smaller and more bird-like, his face flushed and wet with sweat. He stopped in front of

167

Jubal Wills.

'My son Michael is gone!' he said, puffing to regain his breath. 'You have to help!'

'Don't be a fool,' York told him. 'The boy could just have ridden out to hunt.'

The hotel clerk's bald head shook, and he whimpered, a strangling, moaning sound. 'He was milking in our barn,' he said. 'The Fishers next door saw the youngest Troller go inside. Clifton. When my wife called Michael in to eat, both of them were gone.'

CHAPTER FIFTEEN

'He's lyin',' Farnley Troller called from his cell. 'He's tryin' to make trouble for us.'

'He's damnedwell makin' trouble for himself!' Longstreet snapped hatefully. 'He tries somethin' like this!'

Austin stared from Jubal to the Trollers. 'Please, I don't want trouble.'

'We should form a posse, Mayor,' Jubal said. 'Ramon, you can help pass the word to the town men.'

Longstreet cursed. 'What are you going to do, go after our family 'cause his son's left town? You got no proof!'

'That's right!' Farnley's doubled fist

168

pounded the iron bars and he pointed at Austin. 'You're tryin' to get even for somethin! You'll pay, mister! Nobody's come in and said they saw Clifton leavin' with your kid!'

Everett York stepped closer to the hotel clerk. 'Maybe we better wait until we *are* sure, Curtis. The trouble is already bad enough.'

'I'm forming a posse,' Jubal told everyone in the room. 'Ramon, have each man you can find gather out front.' He swallowed the last of the steak and lifted a Winchester from the rack. He checked its lever and then leaned against the desk while he opened the drawer for a box of cartridges. Hall was right about his needing rest. Now that he was on his feet he felt weak, as though his strength slowly drained out of him. He faced the hotel clerk. 'You'll come along?'

'Yes, I will.'

'You sonovabitch!' Farnley yelled. 'You're settin' up our kin! You'll regret it! This town will!'

'I think we should wait,' York began. 'The law...'

'We'll form up at the rail.' Jubal's hand went to the bandages on his face and head. 'Mayor, we'll wait for you to swear us in. You should be with us, Mr. York. You want to be sure the law's handled right. Ride up front

169

with me.'

★ ★ ★

Crossing the boardwalk, Jubal looked westward. Sunlight that slanted through the breaks in the clouds took the grayish color from the flat, the light reflecting sharply off the wet leaves of the cottonwoods and aspens along the curves of the Calligan. With more wind-blown cloud thinning, the sun's glare shone bright-white on the high sandbars and the far stretch of grass. Even with the clear view Jubal could not see a thing that moved, no man or bird or animal. The heat hadn't settled, yet now in his weakened condition it seemed he sweated from every pore.

He slowed in mid-street and glanced around at the closed door of the office. Ramon went into Deistal's restaurant. Austin headed for the hotel. The clerk called to three men near the saddlery, shifting his run toward them when they motioned that they did not understand what he said.

Lew Halstead opened the general store's front door. Jubal told him about the posse, ending with, 'I'd rather have you and Tenney stay here. If they took Austin's son, they'll be after Peter.'

'I've got to open my barn,' the hostler

170

answered. 'I'll have Ramon saddle extra mounts if you need them.'

Beyond the top of the staircase, Myron Stone came out of the spare room. Peter McClain appeared in the doorway behind the heavy-set storekeeper. The boy's face showed surprise, then fear when he saw the deputy's bandaged face and head.

'That shooting was at you last night,' the storekeeper said. 'They won't stop now, Jubal.'

'They're going to be stopped.' The deputy told him of Farnley locked inside the jail, and about Austin's son. While Jubal spoke, Peter came closer. The boy did not shift his stare from the bandages.

'Keep Peter inside the room,' Jubal said. 'They got away with taking Michael. They could try to break in.'

It was Peter who answered. His eyes showed his fear, and hurt. 'I made you be shot. I did it.'

Jubal looked at the boy. 'No, not you.'

'I did. If I didn't come...' He drew in a quick breath, holding back tears. 'You were shot after you helped me and my father.'

'No,' Jubal repeated. He could hear shouts outside the building, and the hard flat-footed clop-clop horses made on the hard pack. He balanced the carbine in his left hand and

171

gripped the boy's shoulder, the fingers holding lightly. 'I wear a badge, and these things happen.'

Peter shook his head, did not answer.

'There are men who hate,' Jubal said. He leaned down closer to the young face, gauging the child for his depth of understanding. He made the boy look into his face. 'You can't stop some men from hating, Peter. I can't explain it. But men like that live on hate. You aren't to blame. Certainly not you.'

He could feel the tenseness calm in the boy. Peter nodded.

'Do what Mr. Stone tells you. Don't leave this store. It will be over soon, and you'll be all right.'

Again Peter nodded. He tried to smile. Jubal straightened.

Myron Stone followed the deputy to the top stair. 'I'm not opening today,' the storekeeper said. 'I'll stay with him. Paul Tenney is going to stay in my storeroom.' His round jowls tightened. 'I won't open up 'til Peter is safe.'

Behind Myron in the doorway, Peter seemed very small to Jubal. 'He'll be safe,' he said.

From the aisle between the counters he could see the horses and men lined two- and three-deep at the jail hitchrail: two of the Ashwoods, Ramon with Jubal's gelding, Gil

Joyce, Bill Flannagan, Phil Lashway, York, Deistal, and a man named Chadwick who had moved into the town only a week ago. Curtis Austin and two others trotted their mounts in from Cross Street. All wore gunbelts and had rifles or carbines in their saddle scabbards, a few of the sixteen with weapons balanced across their saddle horns. The excitement they had built up could be felt. Jubal saw it in their eager narrowed faces, in the way the riders let their horses pivot but held their heads up, keeping them in close.

'The mayor will give the oath,' Jubal called. And when the movement and talk quieted, 'We might be out a while, so—'

'This might cause a fight,' Everett York's voice cut in. 'You family men should know.'

Talk broke out. Most of the men showed anger, wanting to start. Jubal looked at York. The Council member did not add to his statement. He sat in his saddle and waited. In the jail doorway Oakley Hall was also watchful and silent.

Jubal's stare flicked again to York. 'We might strike a fight, as Mr. York says,' the deputy told the men. His gaze swept across the faces. 'Could be rainy, like last night. If any of you feels he should bring extra rain gear, drop back after you're sworn in. You'll catch up.'

173

No answers. Each man waited.

The mayor moved down to the rails while Jubal climbed onto his gelding. Hall had the men recite the oath. Austin was the first to ride out of the press. Singly and in pairs, the posse members swung into loose order after him.

Jubal kneed the gelding ahead. He pulled in at the lead beside Austin and glanced back to where Myron Stone stood on the general-store porch. There was a small shadow in the window behind the storekeeper, Peter McClain staring out, watching them leave.

*　　*　　*

The posse stayed together, riding as one group through the business district. Sun streams that struck the men and horses made the metal on the guns and parts of the harnesses flash. The damp wind flapped the rider's coats and hatbrims and whipped up the horses' manes and tails.

Jubal shivered from the chill. Passing the west-end homes, he smelled bread baking, and coffee and frying ham. He realized his weakness made him hungry, and he threw off the thought. He breathed in and straightened his shoulders and studied the sod for the hoof and shoe tracks the Trollers' horses would have left if they had swung off the road.

The others read the signs as easily. Their mounts, after standing and waiting during the form-up, strained to be let out and run. One or two near the front began to gallop. The men behind called for them to be held down and not to throw mud and clods of the soggy turf.

One voice shouted above the others. Fred Ashwood kicked his mount forward to swing it alongside the deputy and York.

'Out there.' He pointed at the river. 'In the brush, Jubal. There's someone coming into the open.'

A half-mile west, where the high north bank curved in the riffles, a man appeared. Mist streamed out of the screen of timber, a thin transparent whiteness that shifted and drifted in the breeze. The man, who raised one arm to wave, was etched darkly against the mist.

'It's Michael!' Curtis Austin cried. 'It's my son! It's Michael!'

'He is Michael,' York said. He glanced around at the other men. 'It's Austin's son. He doesn't look like he's been hurt.'

Jubal spurred the gelding. The talk stopped among the posse members. Each man was able to recognize Michael Austin now. He was a tall, lanky boy of seventeen, one of the quietest of the town. He ran to meet the riders, flushing meadowlarks from the grass as the horses flushed the small birds, making them flutter up from their cover to sweep and turn high in the air.

Jubal, Austin, and York pulled in near the boy. The others crowded around, jockeying to form a circle so they could hear. Michael had not been harmed. There wasn't a mark on him. His face was red from his run.

'What were you doin'?' his father snapped at him. 'Leavin' without tellin' your mother.'

'I had to leave,' Michael answered. 'Cliff Troller made me go. He had your pistol. He made me ride double with him and took me out to his cousins and his grandfather.' He turned and pointed past the bend of the river. 'We met back there.'

'They didn't hurt you?'

'They didn't touch me. The grandfather sent me to tell Mayor Hall he wants to make a trade. He has something you want, he said, and you've got something he wants.' He looked at Jubal Wills. 'He said you'd know what he meant, Deputy.'

Jubal asked, 'He tell you where he was heading?'

The boy shook his head. 'He'll send word into town. He told me to tell the mayor. He'll tell what he wants.'

Jubal asked, 'What way did they head?'

'Wait, Deputy,' Everett York cut in. 'He was told to tell Mayor Hall, not you. You don't decide on this.'

'Did you see where the Trollers headed?' Jubal asked Michael.

'They followed the river, but I know where they're going. I heard the old man talk about a shack. It can only be Prescott's old rock cabin.'

Jubal nodded. 'They've got the Pruitts,' he said to the men. 'I think they're holding Mr. Dillon, too. Maybe others. Freemont Prescott's cabin is less than three miles from here. It's exactly what they would need.' He pictured the stone building on the north side of the valley, irritated at himself for not thinking of it before, and not acting. 'We have a chance of stopping them from moving anyone out of the valley.'

'You can't try,' York said. 'We should wait for Troller to send word.'

'We can take them if we move fast enough,' the deputy said. He scanned the circle of men, their faces rough and strong and serious, their eyes narrowed and heads bent forward, partly against the wind, but mainly to listen. Their horses were as restless, the need to move strong in them, some chopping at the sod with their hoofs, others lifting and tossing their

177

heads so the clink of the bits and strain of leather mixed with the soft, uneasy thudding.

'We can take them,' Jubal repeated. 'You men know the land and timber near the cabin. They can't run once we move in around them.'

'The boy said Troller will send word to the mayor.' York's voice was loud. His eyes flicked around him to judge the men. He saw the same anger as Jubal saw. 'Deputy, you haven't the authority.'

Jubal motioned to Michael Austin. 'You can ride double with your father.' He looked northward where the grassy meadow stretched open and level until the country tipped up close to the foothills. They would have to circle the cabin to keep the Trollers from reaching the cover of mountain timber or the ravines or dry washes that cut through at various angles close to the rim.

'We'll move in careful,' he warned. 'I don't want to lose one man. No one acts until I say to.' He repeated the order.

'Not one move until I tell you.'

CHAPTER SIXTEEN

Riding at a gallop jolted Jubal. His head ached with a dull throb above his ear, but he could stand it. He had waited for this: they finally closed in on the Trollers. The trouble, the family's viciousness and hate and killing, was close to being ended. He watched to catch some sign of movement which could show Andrew had left a lookout. The timber was too thick for him to spot a man. High above them the mountains rose jagged against the breaks in the clouds. Patches of snow along the far peaks reflected white over the black line of the pines. The nearer peaks of the Madisons that had made Freemont Prescott first build on a high-sheltered bench close to the windbreaks of stone and timber seemed to loom up higher and straighter than they actually were, right against the bluish stretches of the moving sky.

The men of the posse knew the spot as well as Jubal. The Crows and Blackfeet had been active in the first years Prescott had come from Maine to settle. He had chosen the grassy bench for its safety, and had constructed the cabin of stone for protection. After the Indian threat faded, Prescott built his ranch four miles west on the flat. He had allowed the cabin and its wooden barn to be used as a stopover for the valley men who went hunting, or when a town family went camping. Andrew Troller had chosen wisely, with ample game and water from the mountain stream which ran past the cabin. Ten- and twelve-inch squaw and lodgepole pines ringed the buildings on three sides and, along with stands of ash and box elders that skirted the watercourse, offered cover for horses.

Where the flat ended, Jubal raised his hand and stopped. Boulders and rocks from a fall dotted the brush. The horses could slip and stumble on the loose ground. Despite the wind, hoofs clicking on stone might be heard, or the animals' snorts or the slap of leather and jingle of bits would give away their approach.

The men edged in to listen. They were underneath the wind. Jubal did not have to speak loudly. His hand counted out half of the riders, splitting the group.

'Fred Ashwood will lead you eight,' he said. 'You'll swing wide around behind the buildings and be ready to go in from there.'

'My boy?' Curtis Austin asked. 'He hasn't a horse or gun.'

'We're going in on foot,' Jubal told him. He looked at Michael. 'You'll stay with the horses. Keep them out of sight.'

'They'll get skitterish if there's shooting,' Michael said.

'Tie them and hold them. If the Trollers try to run, we'll drive them away from you.'

Jubal mapped out the plan of attack, and could feel the prickle of excitement and damp of sweat along his spine. The remembrance of other days was in his mind, of other plans and orders, when the darker faces of men were close and giving him their attention. 'I'll call to them,' he said at the end. 'None of you leave cover until I give the word. I'll be the first to move.'

'They could spot us closing in,' Everett York said. 'If we lose a man, it's our responsibility.'

'It's my responsibility, Mr. York. I'm issuing the orders. I'll answer for them.'

York closed his mouth, his face still dissatisfied. He waited for Jubal to continue.

'Keep your eyes and ears open,' the deputy warned. 'If they decide to fight, stay behind cover.' With the others, he began to swing down from the saddle.

The seven with Fred Ashwood moved from sight into the woods. Jubal hung back and gave orders about how those who stayed alongside him were to spread out. He kept his body low under the wet pines, careful to make no noise. The forest rose steeply from the grassy bench, and the mountain could no longer be seen. Jubal could feel its shape as he felt the presence of the men inside the cabin, the granite cliffs rolling up and up, leaning away from him and reaching toward the sky.

As distance spread between the men, he could see only Everett York and Curtis Austin. Their footfalls made soft sounds on the pine needles.

He worried now that he hadn't covered the plan completely enough. He was not sure enough what the men would do once shooting started. These were not trained cavalry troops. Each man had a family which needed and depended on him. What if he didn't bring them back alive and safe? If he did lose one of them? His head throbbed, but the nagging worry concerned him more. He would be the one to take the first chance. He'd draw any fire to himself, and the others were to keep their cover. He had made that clear.

The rock cabin was in sight, and the wooden barn. A slight haze of smoke showed from the cabin chimney. Jubal crouched lower, wondering if the closed doors and windows hid a waiting gun, or if Andrew Troller had someone spotted deeper in the woods and even in the trees. He glanced up and around him. York made a scuffing noise as he sprawled flat behind a lodgepole trunk. Jubal heard the hammer of the land agent's carbine click. Jubal's head was clear, he didn't notice the throb, his senses keen.

He raised the Winchester and pressed the stock into his shoulder, bracing the weapon in the prone position. There was a twitch through his ear when he opened his mouth to call.

'Troller, the cabin is surrounded!' His voice echoed through the clearing, up into the timber. 'Open the door!'

No answer was shouted back to him. The cabin door and windows remained shut. And the barn door.

'Troller, we want the people you're holding! Open up and come out! All of you!'

No sound—He could see hoof prints dug into the drying mud in front of the door, and many tracks near the barn. Someone whispered to Jubal's left. Then silence again.

'Troller, I'm coming in! Open up!'

Jubal stood, still hidden by the thick tree trunk. 'Stay down,' he said to York. He repeated the order to Austin on his left. 'Stay down. Pass the word.'

Jubal stepped into the open. He watched the cabin door, the windows, the barn door, waiting for one or more to be thrown open and weapons to fire. He expected it.

The cabin remained silent. The barn was as quiet.

Jubal reached the front door. He lifted his booted foot and kicked, slamming the door wide open, his carbine leveled, ready.

The noise of the door banging the rock wall died. The men appeared from the trees and approached the cabin and barn. The cabin was empty. Coals still burned in the fireplace. The single room was scantily furnished: four bunks next to the side walls, six rawhide-bottom chairs, shelves in one corner, a table. Dishes on the table had the remains of food in them. Coffee had been left half-finished in one mug.

Curtis Austin met Jubal as he stepped outside. York spoke to three of the men near the trees. The Council member's head turned when a voice shouted from the barn. 'Nothin' in here. Horses were stabled, but they're gone.'

Jubal studied the ground. The hoofmarks were plain between the barn and cabin. The trail led into the forest. Up behind the barn. 'They haven't been gone ten, fifteen minutes,' the deputy said.

'No, we aren't following them,' Everett York said. 'They know we've come. They could be waiting.'

'We've lost the surprise,' Austin agreed.

184

'We could lose men. I could lose my boy.'

The men talked among themselves. One or two shook their heads, but most agreed with York and Austin, a few grumbling now.

'We should go back to town,' York said. 'We'll be sent word on what Troller wants. If they have Dillon and the Pruitts, they could harm them now they've been warned.'

'They could,' someone said. Other men nodded their heads.

'Deputy, it's too much of a chance.'

Jubal looked at the faces. His stare moved to the forest, thick and dark and full and covering the immense rearing shadow that was the mountain. A thousand hiding places were up there, trails, ravines, and ledges, and huge rocks which could cover as many men who lay and waited, and sighted with rifles and carbines.

'We'll go back,' he said. 'I want to check the barn, and we'll head home.'

CHAPTER SEVENTEEN

'We were wrong to go out there,' Everett York said. Standing at the hitchrail, he raised his voice louder than he had to speak for Oakley Hall to hear him from inside the jail doorway.

York wanted the Trollers inside the cells to know exactly how he felt, as well as the people of Yellowstone City, and Deputy Jubal Wills. 'He was wrong to lead us.'

The mayor scanned the riders who had dismounted only minutes ago. Some of the older, stiff-legged from being in the saddle half the morning, moved off with their families. Others waited beyond the boardwalk. Two of the young men glanced around at the rest of the posse, another rubbed his stubbled jaw. It was not York who delayed them, but uncertainty, and partly doubt about whether or not they should again be heading out.

'We should have a Council meeting,' York said to Hall. 'We have to decide once and for all.'

'You found tracks,' Hall said. 'They had been using the cabin.'

York shook his head. 'But we could've been shot. They could've killed some of these men. As a Councilman, I have to think of what's best.'

'You didn't get shot,' Hall answered flatly. He stared at Jubal Wills, the deputy quiet and looking tired and drawn since he had swung down from his horse. 'The tracks showed the horses headed into the mountains?'

'They did,' the deputy told him. 'We

186

should go after them. We can trail them.'

'We'd have men killed if we tried to take those hostages,' York said, his voice even louder. 'That's what they are, hostages.'

'If we quit,' Jubal said, 'they can take other hostages. We'd have to do exactly what they want to get them free.'

'And I'd do what they want.' York swung around and glanced from face to face. 'You're wrong. We should wait and learn what they ask and then decide.' His eyes returned to Hall. 'I'll have Morrell and Duncan at my office, and Harold Shanks. I want a vote.'

Hall's heavy-set body did not move. He had seen how the women had waited the entire morning for the posse to return. Now they held onto their husbands, sons, and brothers, standing alongside the horses. One wife tugged at her man's arm. She tried to say something, but he would not answer. He simply shook his head short, his face set, his attention on the deputy and Councilman. Their small daughter pressed close to her mother and father. She was ready to cry. Waiting for so long with the women, hearing their talk of worry and concern, the child had a fear she didn't even understand.

'We should wait,' the mayor said to Jubal. 'We'll get word, and we'll decide how to handle it.'

Jubal exhaled. He saw what Hall saw in the people. The few who would be willing to join another posse were not enough. The wind had died on the ride back. He felt the heat more. The sky was clear. The mountains had changed too. Under the clouds they were dark and heavy, like they crouched against the land. Now they were tall and shining and so immense, a posse could take days just to pick up a trail that might lead anywhere.

'We'll wait,' Hall repeated. 'You rest, Jubal. Ramon will spell me. And Fred Ashwood.'

Clothing brushed clothing while the crowd turned away. The creak of leather and soft chop of hoofs merged with the footsteps. York stayed alongside the mayor. The meaning behind the land agent's narrowed eyes and tight mouth were as clear to Jubal as his argument had been.

Jubal started across Grant. An urge for haste rode him, to get away from the mayor as well as from York. He had believed Hall would listen to him. He hadn't reckoned on York's talk, or the people wanting to get out of the trouble. A few hung on along the walks, mostly men watching the flat, but it was clear what it meant to lose the people . . .

York's stare followed the deputy. 'We made a mistake,' he told Oakley Hall. 'I'm sure we did.'

The mayor looked at him.

'To give that man so much authority,' the Councilman went on. 'It's too much for what he is.' His small, bony head shook to emphasize his sureness. 'We'll take it up at the meeting, and vote, and he'll be all through.'

★   ★   ★

Jubal knew York's thoughts. He had known on the long ride from the cabin. The Council member had hung back behind the deputy and had spoken first to one man, then to another man, and then another. Jubal's hope had been Yellowstone City's mayor. Oakley Hall's sense of duty and responsibility had made an impression on Jubal. Hall had been the first of the Council to back George Dillon's traveling more than a thousand miles down to the Ninth Cavalry encampment in Texas to make his offer. It was why Jubal had taken the lawman's badge. Partly, it was...

The remembrance of Ellie Mae, of how he had talked with her of his leaving the army to put on the lawman's badge, flashed through his mind. He would go to their home after this was finished. Andrew Troller had to act. Word had been sent through Michael Austin, and the old man would not fail in his own

189

sense of duty and responsibility.

Jubal paused on the general store steps. No horse or rider was in sight. One would come. The grandfather was like a hostile chief, never betraying his own. Maybe that's what he had done to himself, Jubal thought. Maybe he had known all along in some deep corner of his mind this had to come, with Hall and anyone in his position making the decision to stand with men who believed like York, and he had betrayed himself hoping otherwise.

But he still wore the badge. He would be the one to face the Trollers. He would not give that up. He hesitated for one final moment while Lew Halstead opened the front door.

'Mister Wills!'

Peter McClain shouted the name. The boy ran along the aisle between the counters, grinning at Jubal. 'You came back! I'm glad!' He hurried to the doorway and looked out into the street. 'Everybody came back safe!'

'Don't stand in the open.' Jubal pushed the boy aside and shut the door. 'You know better than to let yourself be seen.'

'I'm glad you're safe.' Peter still grinned, uncertain now. 'I didn't mean to do anythin' wrong.'

'You're wrong to show yourself. Who told you you could leave the room?'

'Mr. Stone. He didn't lock the door.'

'You can't show yourself. A man with a good aim could shoot you, even from behind a building.'

'I just wanted to see you.' Near tears, the boy shook his head. 'I know how they can shoot. I just was glad to see you.' He turned and started toward Myron Stone, who came down the stairs.

'Peter,' Jubal said.

The boy stopped and stared around, looking so unhappy Jubal had to smile. He walked to Peter and motioned toward the rear of the store.

'I'm going to lie down. You can help me by fixing the blanket on the cot.'

Peter sniffed. 'I can make a whole bed. Mr. Stone taught me.'

'Just the blanket is enough. Smooth it so I can rest.'

'I will. You're not mad at me?'

'No. Remember about showing yourself. You won't be safe until we stop those men.'

Jubal watched the boy nod and then turn and sprint past Myron Stone. The storekeeper's serious glance switched from Peter to the door at the back of the room. He looked as seriously at the deputy.

'Tenney is out behind the storeroom,' he said. 'In case anyone tries to break in.'

'They could,' Jubal told him. 'The old man

will try . . .'

The outbreak of noise and shouts beyond the porch stopped him. Hoofbeats thumped in the street, wagon wheels jounced and ground loudly into the sand. Through the window Jubal saw the buckboard and its driver bent forward on the seat to turn the horse toward the jail. It was Billy Pruitt, his hat pulled low on his forehead. Billy straightened with the reins gripped tight in one hand. The other hand waved away those who crowded off the walks and porches and called questions to him.

Oakley Hall peered out through the jail window. Before the sheriff's office door opened, Jubal stepped onto the store porch. Billy spotted the deputy and immediately swung again into mid-street, his arm and hand beckoning to Jubal.

Jubal couldn't hear every word that was yelled. He saw the blankets in the buckboard bed and the unconscious body that was wrapped in the blankets on the floorboards. He knew it was George Dillon even though the sheriff's head was covered by a bloody red bandage.

Men started to unhook the tailboard to reach the sheriff. Billy waved them off, shouting. His face was pale and drenched with sweat. He gave up the attempt to hold down

192

the people; he tried only to break through the questioning, tightening crowd that bunched together and threatened to keep him from going close to the general store.

'. . . and carry him to Doc's!' he shouted. 'I gotta get back outside town!' He held the reins straight up, controlling the horse. He shoved his wide-brimmed hat clear of his eyes and raised his voice above the others.

'They want you, Deputy!' he cried. 'The Trollers sent me in for you and the two of their family you're holdin! And the kid they came to get!'

'Dillon's bad!' a man yelled. He gripped the sheriff's leg to help slide the body clear of the tailboard. 'They must've tried to kill him.'

'His head's split!' another said. 'They did this?'

'They hit him!' Billy told the upturned faces. 'Ma tried to stop the bleedin' but couldn't. They sent him in . . .'

'We'll get them! They won't get away with is!'

'Damn right! There's enough of us here!' The mob began to move.

'No! No, you can't do anythin'!' Billy pleaded. He watched the men carry Dillon, and the rest of those who pushed and shoved to break away. 'They're holdin' my mother and sisters! They'll kill them! They sent the sheriff in so you'd know they mean what they say! They want to trade for your prisoners, and they want to leave without being followed!' His gaze swept from the people to Jubal and the store doorway. 'You take the prisoners out, Deputy! They want that boy with you!'

'Where are the Trollers now?' the deputy asked.

'The other side of the river, waitin'! I gotta go back!'

'We can take them!' a voice interrupted. 'Enough of us can circle them!' Another man started to join in and agree.

Billy swung around. 'You can't! They'll kill Ma and my sisters! They will! I have to ride out and tell them you'll trade and they won't be followed!' He stared at Jubal. 'You have to come! Alone!' he continued in a voice high and cracking from being forced. 'You can't let them die! Please!'

Oakley Hall reached the wagon with Everett York directly behind him. The horse, skitterish from the excitement and being crowded, jerked its neck to one side and switched its tail. The mayor took hold of the bit. 'Come inside, Billy,' he said. 'We'll talk this out.'

'There ain't time. I had five minutes to leave Mr. Dillon and tell you.' He tightened the reins to free the horse. 'I have to be with Ma and the girls when they're traded. I've got to let them know they'll be all right!'

'No, wait,' Hall began. 'It can be settled.'

'It can't any other way, Mayor! Only their way!'

Hall looked toward Dillon's body. His mouth opened, but York cut him off. 'The boy's right!' He spread both of his arms and motioned for the people to open a path. 'Billy will go back. The deputy has to try. We've got the sheriff. We don't care about the prisoners, only about the woman and her daughters.'

Someone behind the Council member called out to argue.

York turned on the crowd. 'You want them killed? You saw what they did to Dillon!' His voice screaming, he glared to seek out the speaker's face. 'The deputy has to try! He's wearing the badge! The woman and girls for the two prisoners! I say they go!'

The people grew instantly silent, the men's faces strained and thoughtful, the women frightened watching their men. Fear rode them now, after they had seen Dillon and fully realized the threat. The horror of what could happen spread through the entire gathering.

'Please!' Billy begged. 'Let me leave! I promised to go back! I can't let Ma and my sisters be murdered!' He jerked the reins and

195

forced Hall to release the bit. Tears streamed down the boy's cheeks, his lips quivering. 'Do what they want, Deputy! Please or we'll all die!'

His horse reared and bumped the onlookers. The wagon struck others while the animal turned. Hall edged away. He looked up at the deputy on the porch.

'Come to the jail,' the major said to Jubal.

The deputy stayed as he was for another few moments. The men who carried George Dillon had reached Doctor Hobson's office. The buckboard rolled free of the people. Its noises faded. In the following silence, Jubal heard the scuff of a shoe behind him. Myron Stone and Lew Halstead blocked the doorway. Jubal could not see Peter McClain's face, just the boy's shoes and the bottom of his legs standing inside the store protected by the men.

'Lock up and stay in there,' he told them. He went down the steps to cross toward the jail.

*   *   *

Oakley Hall said, 'We need more time.'

At the gunrack Jubal kept his back turned to the mayor. In his mind he could see George Dillon's slack face and bloody bandaged head.

He pictured the Pruitts—Billy, his mother, and the small girls—while he listened to Hall and York exchange arguments. The discussion grew more confused when the other town officials, Shanks, Morrell and Duncan, hurried across the threshold and came inside.

Jubal had the Greener loaded. He had extra shells in his pocket. He tucked the heavy shotgun under one arm, then drew his .44 Colt and spun the cylinder. His pulse thumped in his veins, not painfully, but a different feeling somehow, something that calmed and satisfied him.

'You shouldn't go out,' Hall repeated. 'Not alone, Jubal.'

'He has to,' York said. 'He knows his duty. It's what everyone expects of him.' The three other Councilmen nodded. The four looked quickly into the cell block as Farnley Troller spoke.

'We better be let free,' the prisoner warned. 'Grandpa'll finish off them people. It won't be pretty. You can damnwell believe that!'

'What are you waitin' for?' Longstreet Troller questioned. 'You scared to leave this town, Deputy?'

Jubal took a step toward the cells. Ramon Lerrazza said, 'I will come. With both of us . . .' Alongside him Fred Ashwood's voice was louder. 'Three of us, Jubal. I'll back you, too.'

Jubal shook his head. He motioned with the weapon's heavy double barrels for the prisoners to walk in single-file from the cell block. In the first cell Joe Jack coughed. His dark face grimaced hatefully. He spat at the deputy's boots.

'You're doin' the white man's rotten work,' he snarled. 'You know what you'll get for it.'

Jubal prodded Farnley with the barrels to have him step faster toward the gunrack. He motioned for both men to halt beyond the reach of the rifles and carbines.

'You should work for your own,' Joe Jack snarled louder. 'You won't get anythin' from doin' their dirty work.'

'I wouldn't get it taking your way.' The deputy stared down into the dark face. 'None of us will.'

Farnley swung around on the deputy. 'You're not connectin' him to us. You have to let us go.'

Jubal did not answer. He reached up to a wall peg and took down a coiled lariat. He loosened the noose and slid it over Farnley's neck. When he reached again to take a second rope, Longstreet edged away.

'You got no right doin' this. We're not being strung up.'

'Yes, he's right,' York began. 'They're not being held . . .'

'That's enough,' Jubal said. 'There hasn't been a vote on my badge. I can have one more man come with me, Mr. York.'

York sputtered. He remained silent while the deputy led the prisoners to the closed front door.

'Do what I say,' Jubal told the Trollers. 'I'm holding the lines. One move by you, either of you, and a good yank will break your necks.'

Both men nodded.

The lines gripped in one hand, the Greener shotgun in the other, the deputy motioned with the twin barrels at the knob.

'Open it.'

Men waited together on the boardwalk: five young men and two of the older town citizens. David Ashwood stood at the front with Michael Austin. They edged aside to allow the prisoners to step onto the thick planks. Dave spoke for the group.

'We want to help,' he said. 'Give us guns, Deputy.'

'No. I have to do this alone.'

'I should be with you,' Michael Austin told him quickly. 'I saw what they did to Mr. Dillon.' He stared into Jubal's face. 'Deputy, the man who shot your wife was in the hotel with the Trollers. My father told me.' He pointed at Farnley. 'He wasn't in the hotel either when you were shot or when McClain was killed.' His thin head moved up and down in a nod, as though he were a part of the trouble and had been a part of it from the beginning. 'Pa was scared for us, for my mother and us kids. I have to be with you.'

Jubal shook his head. 'Stay here, all of you.' He was aware of a return of the feeling he'd had while he loaded the Greener, the absence of pain in the pulsebeat along his wound, the same satisfied and expectant and hopeful something in the sensation that coursed through him now.

He moved past the men and off the walk. He kept the two ropes tight in his left hand. The shotgun was balanced so one finger brushed lightly against the triggers.

He trailed the two Trollers along mid-street, thinking of George Dillon barely alive in the doctor's office, of Ellie Mae and their baby, and of Owen McClain, and the men who were responsible for their deaths. People watched from doors and windows. Some were at the mouths of the alleyways, yet Jubal hardly saw them. Individual faces had lost their identity. He didn't recognize anyone. He no longer thought of anyone or anything except what he was going out to do.

CHAPTER EIGHTEEN

Jubal felt the heat of the sun. It was higher and brighter, its burn striking him like a hammer blow. He had to squint against the glare to see across the flat to the timber along the river.

That's where the Trollers waited, he was sure, the five of them hidden somewhere in the screen of brush and trees. He breathed in and squared his shoulders, pacing Longstreet and Farnley.

The people would crowd into the street, Jubal knew, after he and his prisoners moved from one block to another and out past the big, finer homes. No one could help him. With the sheriff so bad off, dying for all he knew, it was up to him as lawman. Michael Austin's telling him Joe Jack had been with the Trollers had numbed him. Andrew's lies, all the constant denials, were jeering insults. The truth made his every throb and soreness ache with fury; it reminded him there were others besides Dillon and his own who had been hurt. The boy, Peter, had lost so much. Jubal hadn't looked toward the general store window. Yet he felt the boy there with Myron Stone and Lew Halstead, watching him leave.

He wouldn't fight the Council, not a five-man vote which would be stacked against him. The town wasn't that much, hot as the gates of hell in summer, and so cold in winter a man or cattle could be frozen stiff in minutes. Myron's store was like the other buildings, the paint sun-blistered and wind-peeled, the boards so beaten and dried by blown sand they were scoured down to a grayness that made them seem old and worn... He was glad Myron and Halstead had blocked him from looking into the boy's face on the porch. Peter lost if he lost, and now he did not dare to glance around and see him again...

Farnley and Longstreet shifted their step to head toward the livery and stage-line work area. Halstead's handyman had opened the barn's high front doors. The hostler led the Trollers' two horses past a Montana-Dakotas Concord coach. Both mounts were fresh and saddled. The smell of the stables rode on the hot air, of leather and hay and manure, and the good clean animal smell.

Jubal jerked the ropes. 'Stay in the road,' he ordered. 'Keep going.'

Farnley gagged. 'We need our horses.'

'They'll be sent out. Keep walking.'

Neither man could argue with the nooses pulled tighter. Farnley coughed. He stumbled and caught his stride and they moved faster.

Jubal wondered what Peter would do to live, how he would get along . . .

Passing the west-end houses, he wondered what Andrew Troller was going to do. The old man might decide to forget the boy and leave the valley after the trade. His sons walked free, and they would ride out along the trail through the trees and never come back . . . But Jubal knew the family existed too much on hate and did not live with the truth, and they knew even without the badge he would be after them. He thought of the warped way they had held George Dillon, the sheriff's head split and bleeding, then sent him in with the terrified Billy Pruitt. He did not have to wonder about Andrew Troller. He knew . . .

Jubal suddenly gripped the ropes tighter and drew back his hand. The two prisoners halted.

Clifton Troller had stepped from the trees and into plain view. He was a quarter-mile away, yet the deputy could almost make out the expression on his face before he again vanished into the brush.

Farnley's head turned. He stared at the deputy, his eyes bright with excitement and expectation. 'Let us go,' he said. 'We'll send the Pruitts in.'

'Stay like you are,' Jubal told them. 'I'll say what you do when I see your family coming.'

*   *   *

'They're comin'!' Clifton Troller called. He broke from the brush into the small open space among the tall cotton-woods. He raised one arm and pointed at the flat. 'Another couple minutes, Grandpa!'

'The boy with them?'

'No. Only Uncle Longstreet and Farnley. The deputy's walkin' behind them. I think he's got a shotgun.'

Andrew swung about in the saddle, holding his rifle poised to slam at the Pruitts in their buckboard. Billy straightened his body in front of his mother next to him on the seat. He lifted his hand to deflect a blow from his sisters behind him. The two girls did not cry. They stood in the wagon bed, stiff and awkward and frightened, hugging close to their mother and older brother.

'Climb down,' Andrew snarled at the boy. Billy did not move. The grandfather lowered his weapon's iron barrel. His hands shook and he looked as if he wanted to kill. 'Git down with Clifton. They ain't turnin' over all we want. We ain't either.'

Billy hesitated, pressing close to his mother and sisters.

'Down, you was told!' The red-headed Ike Bean leaned his stubby body low in the saddle and grabbed Billy's shoulder. He pulled him away and forced the boy to swing off the step plate.

Alice Pruitt made no motion to stop the men. Her lips trembled. She held the reins gripped in both of her hands and waited with her daughters.

'You *will* let him go?' she said. 'My son for the other boy?'

'That's what we agreed.' The old man's eyes flicked from one grandson to another— Ulysses, Frank, Calem, Clifton—then to Ike Bean, the man's face as grim as each of his family's. But Bean's reddish beard was a reminder he wasn't one of the family, that he took their pay.

'Stay even with us when we ride out,' the grandfather told the woman. 'Start now.'

The buckboard rolled forward. The old man and Ulysses were on one side. The others, with Billy Pruitt and Clifton a few steps behind them, kept as close to the wagon's opposite sideboards.

Andrew Troller cursed the instant they were in the open. He saw that nobody followed the deputy and his prisoners. And he

205

saw the ropes and the nooses the deputy held tightened about each neck.

'Sonovabitch!' he screamed. 'You black sonovabitch nigger!'

★ ★ ★

The words stung like a whiplash. Jubal felt the impulse to begin shooting. He'd lived in the town all these months and no one had as much as whispered such words. The Council members wanted his badge, his job, but they hadn't thrown insults. Jubal halted thirty feet from the brush. He drew up on the ropes and jammed the barrels into one Troller spine, then the other.

'Stop,' he ordered. Longstreet and Farnley obeyed.

'The boy!' the grandfather was shouting in a string of curses. 'You was supposed to bring him! You didn't bring him!'

'That's close enough,' the deputy called. 'Pull up. Don't come closer.'

The grandfather yanked back on the reins. The riders and wagon stopped beyond the trees two hundred feet away. Jubal's eyes swept across the faces, Clifton and two more Trollers and the redhead with Billy, Andrew and the other grandson on the far side of Alice Pruitt and her daughters. They hadn't hidden anyone in the trees to his left, he was sure.

Jubal called, 'Begin when you're ready, Troller.'

Andrew's face was haggard, but in spite of this he breathed confidence. His eyes shone with it. He watched the deputy with a hate that threatened he could kill, that promised it. He gestured with his weapon beyond the deputy and his son and grandson into the town.

'We want McClain!' he shouted. 'You didn't live up to your agreement!'

'We didn't agree,' Jubal answered. He saw the others were as ready to draw and shoot as the old man. Ulysses rubbed one hand along his right thigh. Calem and Frank and the redhead were poised. Clifton was smiling, his hand also at his waist.

'I'm ready,' Jubal added. 'Let Billy climb into the wagon.'

'He does like hell,' Andrew answered. 'You'll die, boy! He will! They all will!' He brought the rifle down, leveling the barrel.

'You crazy?' Farnley yelled. 'Grandpa, don't! Let them go!'

'No, dammit, that black sonovabitch!'

'That's enough,' the deputy shouted. 'I'll take them back. Decide now!' He pulled hard on the ropes.

The nooses tightened around both necks.

Farnley back-stepped but Longstreet screamed. 'They'll hang us, Paw! Curtis told them everythin'! You stop the trade and we'll hang!'

Andrew's bony body was erect in the saddle. He swore and looked at Clifton. He motioned for him to release the boy's shoulder. While Billy climbed onto the seat, the old man snapped more orders. On either side of the buckboard the men edged out to form a line.

A skirmish line, Jubal thought. Wide and solid, ready to come at him. He began to sweat in a chill wetness that made the skin between his shoulders bunch up and crawl.

'I'll start them,' the deputy called across the bare open space. 'You start the wagon.'

'What about the horses?' the old man questioned. 'You didn't bring their horses?'

'They'll be sent out. After we start.'

Longstreet scuffed his boots and nervously turned his head. 'Deputy, you have to loosen the ropes.'

'When they move. You wait, and walk slow.'

'Paw, you want us to live,' Longstreet yelled, 'don't wait any longer!'

Andrew kicked the Pruitt horse. The buckboard rolled forward. Jubal dropped the ropes and gripped the Greener in both of his hands. Farnley and Longstreet took one short step, then another, surer stride. Each man's hands came up to throw off his noose.

'Let them drag,' the deputy told them. 'Until you pass the wagon.' He backed a step, another and another. He was a long gunshot away. The farther he moved the better chance he had.

The wagon picked up speed, its iron-rimmed wheels spewing a shower of dirt and dust over the brown, dry grass. The two Trollers broke into a run now, the ropes dragging and snaking behind them. Jubal stepped backwards faster. The bare open spaced widened. He waved the wagon off. 'Swing toward town,' he warned the Pruitts. 'Don't come near me and make a single target.'

Billy whipped the horse. The rumble and creak and squeaks of the buckboard were loud as it angled away. Jubal clearly heard each word of Billy's voice, as if he were close to him.

'They're goin' to try to get you!' the boy yelled. 'They'll gun you down!'

Jubal had no time to escape. Andrew acted before the shouts were drowned out by the noise of the wagon. He spurred his mount toward Farnley and Longstreet, and his grandsons and Bean moved to stay alongside him. The running men tore at the ropes. They yanked the nooses off over their heads and kept their arms stretched to get weapons into their hands.

Andrew opened fire. A second gun banged, and a third and a fourth. Bullets zinged past Jubal, burned by overhead, exploded bursts of dust at his feet. He made a dash for the river while the shots came faster, the horses' hoofs chopping louder, nearer. Then something that slashed like a whip struck his left thigh and spun his body around in a half circle.

Jubal stumbled. The pain in his leg driving up into his groin was worse than the throb of his head. He was at the edge of the grass, doubled over, pushing branches aside with the shotgun, using the brush and trees to get out of the sights of the men who closed in on him. He tripped and fell. The leg was watery, weak, the pain an agony that squeezed the breath from him so that he had to roll onto his elbows to support the heavy weapon.

Slugs smashed the branches and whacked the tree trunks. Andrew's voice shouted, 'Get him! Circle around him! Watch them out there!' The grandfather's head and upper part of his body came into Jubal's view. Jubal aimed, squeezed the trigger, and with the booming blast rolled deeper into the tangle of grass and brush.

Andrew screamed. Another voice shouted, Farnley's voice, wild and horrified. The rolling of his body saved Jubal. Bullets whipped into the earth at the exact spot he had just left. He rolled again, toward the river.

Farnley ran, twenty feet from him. The rifle he held was pointed at Jubal. Jubal's second shot drove Farnley backward, blowing his body inches off the ground.

All the yells and gunfire weren't in the trees. Jubal thought he heard shouts of voices and more shots coming from a distance. He couldn't listen, couldn't take precious seconds to reload. The Greener was too heavy in his weakness and pain. He dropped the shotgun and rolled over once, again and again and then again, nearer and nearer the river banking.

He struck the trunk of a large cottonwood and stopped. He lay without a movement or a sound and fought down the sickishness and tried to catch his breath. The voice that called to his right was Longstreet's, the other answering at the edge of the trees was Ike Bean's. They were moving fast, cutting in toward him.

Jubal grabbed at his thigh. Before he could grip firmly, the fingers of his left hand slid in the warm blood that drenched his pants. He shook off waves of dizziness, knowing he'd never reach the bank to go over the edge and use the water and river boulders for cover. He had wanted this, had pushed it to draw in the Trollers. He'd thought he was too smart to be cornered alone and caught, too battle-wise, he'd come through too many other fights . . .

He pulled the Colt from its holster. It was too heavy for one hand to aim. He let go of the leg and gripped the weapon with both of his hands. His bloody fingers touched the handle, but they would not hold. Jubal's body strained against the numbing pain. Nauseated, fearful, he whimpered, groaning to force the hand not to slip.

He heard footsteps. The brush parted to his left. A sombrero, then the red-stubbled face and neck and shoulders of Ike Bean appeared through the branches. Jubal's hand gripped, his trigger finger squeezed, banging out a bullet that struck the redhead in the center of the chest.

'He's here! Here!' Longstreet's voice was a scream as he crashed into the high growth of brush, pushed it aside, and charged at Jubal. Jubal's fingers slipped on the handle. He could not aim or fire. He tried to roll away in the fierce hope he would somehow gain time. He looked into the barrel of Longstreet Troller's weapon, the muzzle huge and round and ugly.

'This is for our family,' Longstreet cried crazily. 'You stopped our rights and . . .'

He never heard the explosion that sent a Greener load ripping into him from behind to tear his back and head and face apart.

The full blast of the shotgun kept pounding in Jubal's eardrums even after Longstreet fell. He stared up and saw Ramon Lerrazza standing over the dead man.

'We got the others,' the Mexican said. He lowered the weapon and leaned down to help Jubal Wills stand.

★   ★   ★

Jubal let the Colt drop. A strange expression was on his face, as though he did not believe it was finished and he was alive and whole. He tightened both hands around his thigh. Ramon supported him across his back and under his arms. The ache of his head and groin made him giddy and light on his feet, and he almost lost his balance. Ramon placed the Greener alongside his bad leg, the barrel held muzzle-down for a crutch. He propped Jubal against him, careful of how the deputy tightened his fingers on the wound.

'All of them?' Jubal questioned.

'The young one, we took,' the Mexican told him. 'He did not try to fight alone.'

Past Longstreet and Bean now, Jubal could see through the branches. Five bodies were sprawled on the flat. Men were out there standing near the dead. More headed toward the river from the town. Women and a few children ventured into the open behind them. The Pruitt wagon was stopped beyond the two-story homes, with people gathered around the buckboard seat and wagon bed.

Ulysses and Frank Troller lay in the grass at the edge of the brush. Calem, his head half torn away, was as dead five yards from his grandfather. Andrew Troller's horse cropped at the grass near the old man's body. Jubal paused to stare down at the grandfather. The Greener shot had not hit above his neck. The deep-lined bony face had not been touched. It had a strangely shocked look, the skin the colour of dark-burned leather. The mouth was half open, its white teeth shiny in the bright sun. Blood drenched Andrew's shredded chest and what was left of his shirt and stomach.

'Michael Austin will take Clifton in,' Ramon said.

The youngest Troller stood between his grandfather and the last body of a man on the ground. Clifton had not been wounded. He looked dumbfounded at the viciousness of what had happened, every one of his family

214

dead except himself, everything over and settled so quickly and completely. Jubal saw Fred Ashwood and Oakley Hall bent over the fifth body. Lew Halstead was there, and Curtis Austin.

Jubal relaxed his fingers on his leg and leaned more of his weight on Ramon. Reaction had not clouded any of his thoughts. The satisfaction he felt at the trouble being ended was dimmed by his pain and his own loss. He had no heart-thumping exhilaration within him, only the calm realization that no person would any longer have to live in fear. Peter McClain could come out of the general store, the boy always would be safe... He took a slow step alongside Ramon. Then he hesitated.

The last dead man was David Ashwood. The young, beardless face seemed to be stilled in sleep, until Jubal saw the tiny round dark bullet hole in the hairline above his forehead.

Fred Ashwood turned toward the deputy.

'He was running out with us to help you,' Ramon said quietly. 'He went down as though he had tripped.'

'Fred, I'm sorry,' Jubal said. He shook his head, and Ashwood turned again to his son.

The Ashwoods had been the first to help, Jubal remembered, the father and his sons willing to face everything with him for the others in the town. Why do the good ones have to suffer and die, he thought. Why? He moved on with Ramon. His eyes searched the faces, the men and the women, and the still-excited and frightened expressions of the young. He searched out Everett York. He wanted to talk to the Council member.

Peter McClain stood alone to one side of the crowd, which had strung out from the buckboard. Myron Stone helped the Pruitt girls climb down off the wagon, but Jubal could not see York.

Oakley Hall's voice sounded behind Jubal. 'Deputy, we'll take over until you're able to wear the sheriff's badge.'

Jubal stopped and looked back.

'George Dillon is very bad,' the mayor told him. 'He's lost so much blood. Whatever does happen, he'd want you to hold his badge.'

'There was going to be a vote on me, Mayor.'

'I can tell you about the vote. The others stayed in the jail with the prisoner. You're the man we want, Jubal.'

Those close to the mayor picked up his words and echoed them. Jubal wiped the warm sweat from his forehead. His gaze ran across the faces. He did not have to speak to York. He had made his decision, thinking of George Dillon and of his wife, and now looking at the Ashwoods and Peter McClain.

He stared beyond the people and Yellowstone City's bigger, finer homes. He did want to stay here where his wife and child would always be. The house they had lived in was hidden behind the false fronts and peaks and roofs of the business district. He would go to the undertaker's for Ellie Mae and bring her home. For a while he would be alone with her.

He beckoned to the boy who stood alone. Peter began to run forward.

Jubal waited until the boy reached him. He let go of the Greener and, resting one hand on Peter's shoulder, continued ahead. He intended only to have the boy walk with him, but a sudden weakness made him lean more weight on the small shoulder.

Peter looked up at Jubal's face, his own thin face serious. He tightened his arm about Jubal's good leg, and with Ramon supporting the left side, the two moved with their burden past the people and into the town.

Photoset, printed and bound in Great Britain by
REDWOOD BURN LIMITED, Trowbridge, Wiltshire